Lord Elliott was determined not to be out-flanked. So when he heard female footsteps hurrying toward them, he was on his toes and ready. Perhaps he failed to note that it was Audrey and not Regina who paused beneath the mistletoe. Be that as it may, he acted.

The old Christmas custom seemed to be taking on a brand-new dimension. Perhaps Lord Hunt had set the tone with his performance. If so, Lord Elliott now raised the level several notches. As the kiss went on, the others hardly knew which way to look. For Regina had arrived and was standing beside the oblivious couple still locked in each other's arms.

"My, that does look like fun. . . ."

By Marian Devon
Published by Fawcett Books:

DECK
THE
HALLS

Marian Devon

FAWCETT CREST • NEW YORK

A Fawcett Crest Book
Published by Ballantine Books
Copyright © 1995 by Marian Pope Rettke

Library of Congress Catalog Card Number: 95-90425

ISBN 0-449-22322-1

Manufactured in the United States of America

First Edition: November 1995

10 9 8 7 6 5 4 3 2 1

For Leslie, Sarah, and Stephanie,
first-water diamonds

Prologue

"At a time like this a man needs his family around him."

Sir Jervis Brougham lay back against his pillows and strove to appear pathetic. He was aided in this endeavor by the nightcap and nightshirt he still wore at noon. But a craggy countenance shaped by sixty years of arrogance and a voice tuned to drowning out the baying of his hounds quite failed him. He seemed to realize as much for he tried again. This time there was more quaver and less "view halloo" in his tone.

"Yes, by gad, a cove's family should be gathered around him at a time like this."

His ward, Miss Anne Welbourne, chose to misunderstand him. "Oh, I quite agree, sir. Christmas just isn't Christmas without family."

"Christmas be damned." The baronet glared. "You don't get me meaning. The thing is, I'm on me deathbed."

Miss Welbourne prayed for patience, a commodity not usually in such short supply. But she had just broken off a consultation with Cook to hare up three flights of stairs for the third time in an hour. She took a deep breath. The prayer was answered. Her pretty face remained serene and her voice was soothing.

"You mustn't put yourself into a taking, sir. Dr. Ward says that you are suffering from dropsy and gout. Debilitating, certainly. But he assures me that the condition is by no means life-threatening." Dr. Ward's exact words had been "There's nothing wrong with Sir Jervis but port and lobster patties. The old behemoth will outlive us all. Wouldn't surprise me one bit if he has to be knocked on the head for the Judgment."

The baronet snorted. " 'Dr. Ward says,' " he mimicked. "That old quack wouldn't know his arse from his elbow. I'm the one concerned here and I tell you I'm dying. And I want me family put on notice. Me family." His lip curled. "By God, if I don't feel like that King Lear cove they forced us to read about in school. At the time I couldn't understand what the fellow was on about. But now I know what it's like to be old and stuck with nothing but a gaggle of females for offspring."

Miss Welbourne had opened her mouth to dispute the accuracy of her guardian's last statement, but she quickly reconsidered. Fortunately, Sir Jervis was too engrossed with his train of thought to spy her near indiscretion.

"Yes, b'gad, old King Lear and I are all of a piece. Only in his case it was three daughters he was saddled with and in mine it's two. But then I've a granddaughter besides, so it works out the same. Well, not really," he amended practically, "for you'll only have to write two letters. Regina's in Bath with her mother.

"Want you to fire off the letters right away, Anne. Tell 'em I want 'em here for Christmas. And be sure to tell 'em I'm on me deathbed. Otherwise pistols wouldn't get them to Stonebridge Park. And while you're at it," he mused, "tell Audrey to bring those stepsons of hers. And have Judith bring Regina's fiancé along." He chuckled nastily. "Chained to her chariot wheels, naturally."

"Oh, but do you think that a good idea?" The protest was a mild one that seemed to recognize its own futility.

"I think it's a capital idea!" Sir Jervis thundered. "Got to have somebody in this house besides females. Now hurry on and write the demmed letters. Need to give 'em all time to undo whatever plans they've made. So get on with it." His face softened into what almost passed for affection. "I know you'll do the pretty, child, but the thing is, be sure to stress that I'm on me deathbed."

Anne Welbourne managed to repress her sigh until the bedchamber door had closed behind her.

The click of the latch served as a signal. Sir Jervis slid out of his high four-poster with remarkable alacrity for a man hovering on the brink. He hobbled on his gouty foot across the Aubusson carpet and opened the heavy window hangings that he had expressly forbidden Anne to touch. He seated himself at a writing table situated to catch the light and extracted a sheet of paper. He selected a quill, tested its point, then dipped it into the inkpot. After a moment's hesitation he began scratching and blotting his way from top to bottom of the page. Then, not content with this much communication, he shifted the paper sideways and proceeded to scribble across what he had already written.

"Well, the die is cast," he muttered as he read, with some difficulty, through his efforts. He then signed it with a flourish: Anne Welbourne.

"That ought to put the cat in among the pigeons."

Sir Jervis chuckled as he sprinkled the pressed paper liberally with sand.

Chapter One

THE DOWAGER LADY HUNT SAT FROWNING OVER A letter while her tea and toast grew cold. A former nonpareil now in her middle years, she still laid considerable claim to beauty—and also to style as her deceptively simple round dress of jaconet muslin proclaimed.

The fifth Baron Hunt of Larksdale, one of her companions in the sun-lit breakfast room, watched her uneasily. He was conservatively dressed for the metropolis in a dark superfine coat with pearl buttons, fawn unmentionables, and glossy Hessian boots.

His brother, Captain Lawrence Hunt—Larry to his friends, who were legion—was oblivious to the strained atmosphere. He had lately returned from the Peninsula, where he had served under the Duke of Wellington, and still wore the uniform of the Life Guards while his Bond Street tailor stitched industriously on civilian clothes. He was

5

fond of saying that army food had been worse than the Frogs' and as a consequence was now consuming buttered eggs with relish while washing them down with quantities of ale.

The brothers were twins, but there was little about them to reveal that relationship. Danforth, the elder by ten minutes, often declared that it was only fair he should get the title for Larry had got everything else: height, looks, and charm. And how he had managed to be born first defied all reason, for Larry had been bear-leading him ever since.

The observation was only partly true. The captain did top six feet with a broad-shouldered physique to match, while his brother was a little below average height and slightly built. Larry's hair was a brilliant blond, Danforth's more subdued. Though both were endowed with strong, regular features, there was little facial resemblance between the two. Except for their eyes. Both pairs were of a brilliant blue. They also held in common a deep affection for each other and a protective fondness for the Dowager Lady Hunt.

They had been nine when their father brought home his eighteen-year-old bride. And it was often remarked by those who knew them best that Audrey had not reared the twins, the boys had brought her up. This topsy-turvy relationship had become even more pronounced when, eight years later, the ill-fated fourth baron broke his neck in the hunting field. Four years after that his heir was forced to carry all responsibility for the widow himself when his brother went away to war. He was glad now to share it once again.

"Oh, I say, Audrey." The captain had had his fill of the long silence. He spoke thickly through a mouth full of light wig. "Are you trying to memorize that curst letter? You must have read it a dozen times by now."

"How would you know?" Danforth adroitly snatched the remaining roll from beneath his brother's hand as the captain reached for it. "You've done nothing since you've been home but feed your face. Audrey and I have to be quick off our marks or we'd starve to death entirely." The fact that a footman was replenishing the supply even as he spoke did not lessen the baron's tone of pseudomartyrdom.

"Shame on you, Danforth." Audrey looked up from her letter and frowned. "Larry was a walking shadow when he returned to us. Now look at him," she said admiringly. "He is almost himself again. Another stone will just about do it, I should think."

"Oh, well then. He should easily reach that goal by suppertime. And add a gut and jowls by the New Year."

"Don't you wish." His brother grinned amiably as he helped himself to a slice of thick York ham. "You've had your pick of the ladies while I've been away. But now that little brother's back . . . Nervous, are we?"

"Actually, he hasn't had his pick." Their stepmother sighed. "He certainly might have done. But he has ignored all invitations. Not to mention the lures cast his way. Some by extremely eligible females. Diamonds of the first water included. But you must know that he has always depended upon you to arrange his life. When you left he simply dropped off the face of the earth socially." She frowned down at her letter once again.

"Dull old dog, ain't he? Well, never mind. I'll soon have him—" Larry broke off in midsentence. "Audrey! What the devil is in that thing? Here you are at it again."

She looked up and smiled apologetically. "Oh, I am

7

sorry. It's an invitation. No, a summons. And I don't know what to do for the best. It's from Papa, you see. He wants us to spend Christmas at Stonebridge Park."

"The devil he does!" Danforth put down his fork.

"Us? *Us?*" His brother looked horrified. "If he thinks I'm going to spend my first Christmas back in England in his gothic mausoleum, he much mistakes the matter. I'd as lief holiday in Siberia."

"Write back and tell him we've all got the pox," Danforth suggested.

"I don't think I can do that. Besides," she mused aloud, "it might not be so terrible. I really could do with a change from London."

"A change from London?" Larry gaped at her. "Am I hearing right? It used to be we were never able to pry you away from the metropolis. You hate the country."

"Oh, yes, I know." She looked uncomfortable. "But this is different, you see. Anne writes that Papa says this is bound to be his final Christmas. He is convinced that he is dying."

"You don't say." Larry seemed unmoved by the news. "Doubt that will make him any more lovable. Besides, hasn't he been shuffling off this mortal coil ever since we've known him, Brother?"

"True." The baron nodded. "As I recall, he's used poor health as an excuse to dodge all family responsibility."

"Well, yes," Sir Jervis's daughter agreed. "But this seems different. Anne says he is most desirous of having his family around him." She sighed heavily. "Judith is bound to go. She would never shirk her duty."

"What you mean," Danforth said, "is that she would never risk having the old tyrant cut her off."

Larry pushed aside his plate, suddenly intense.

"Mrs. Fielding's to be there, is she? Do you think she will bring Regina with her?"

"Anne's letter says 'all the family' is to come. Certainly Papa will wish to see his only grandchild."

"Not to mention his only grandchild's only fiancé."

Danforth received a set-down look from his stepmother for this sotto voce remark.

Audrey refolded her letter, a look of resolution on her face. "Yes," she repeated, "I am convinced that it will all work out for the best. I shall go to Stonebridge."

Her stepsons looked at her doubtfully.

"Are you sure that is what you wish?" Danforth asked. "There is the Weston ball, you know. And God knows what else you'll be missing. I wouldn't take the old man's ailments too seriously if I were you. At least wait till after the New Year."

"No, I am quite determined. I shall spend the Christmas holiday in the bosom of my family." She barely repressed a shudder. "But you two need not feel under any obligation. After all, you are not blood relations."

"True. And that very thought will buoy me up all the time we are there."

"You mean to go then?" Danforth looked at his twin suspiciously.

"Wild horses won't prevent it. But as Wicked Stepmother just said, you are under no obligation. Go to the Weston ball by all means."

"The devil take the Weston ball. Weren't you listening? Audrey just said I'm a social disaster. If you two plan to play the martyrs, well, by damn, I'll pack my hair shirt and go along."

"You are quite sure? It is bound to be tedious. And my father actually could be dying, you know, which will make it unbearable. Larry, this is no way to spend your first civilian Christmas."

"Spending it without you here would be a worse fate. Right, brother?"

"Right."

Audrey's eyes misted. "I really don't deserve you two. Well, then." She strove for a businesslike composure as she stood. "Is it settled then?" They nodded. "Very well. I shall write Anne immediately that the three of us are coming."

The twins watched her leave the room.

"Surely you're sufficiently gorged by now," Danforth remarked as his brother replenished his teacup from a porcelain pot decorated with forget-me-nots.

"True. But there is something we need to talk about. And here and now is as good a place and time as any."

"That sounds ominous." Danforth poured himself some tea and tried to make light of his brother's uncharacteristic seriousness. "What's put you in a pucker?"

"I'm not in a pucker. Just say I'm concerned. About Audrey."

"Oh?"

An excellent card player, Danforth was noted for not betraying his emotions. Any uneasiness he might now be feeling was well hidden. "What about Audrey? I haven't noticed anything amiss."

"Mayhap that's because you've been with her all along and the change has come about gradually. But, trust me, she has changed. She was always so lighthearted, full of fun. She's too serious now by half, I'd say. Something's troubling her. I'd stake my life on it. I can't believe you haven't noticed."

"Are you sure there is anything to notice?"

"I just said so, didn't I? I tell you, she is not the same Audrey that I left."

"Well, we are all getting older. And you know how women are about that."

"Fustian. She doesn't look nearly her age. Besides, for a beauty Audrey has always been remarkably unvain. There must be something to account for . . . Oh, I say," a light seemed to dawn, "is she in love?"

"My God, you are a cynic. 'In love'? What a reason to be blue-deviled. And here I'd always thought one was supposed to walk on clouds and so on."

"That shows how little you know. Could be a married cove, for instance. How about it? Is there some man in her life?"

"Droves of 'em, as usual. But one particular one? I don't think so."

"Well, there's a theory smashed. Think hard. What else could account for the change in her?"

For a moment Danforth was tempted to confide in his brother. But only for a moment. For he knew that he and Larry would never see eye to eye on this particular issue. Larry was far too tenderhearted to agree that in the long run he was acting for the best. "Well, she truly is concerned about her father, of course," he equivocated. "The old man may be a rum touch, but he is her father."

"Well, yes. Perhaps." Larry seemed to lack conviction. "There's that, of course. Hate to bring it up because the three of us have always dealt so well together, but ought she to marry again? Maybe that's the problem. After all, we're twenty-four, and though, thank God, I don't have to worry about that sort of thing, you'll soon need to get yourself an heir. That's bound to put Audrey out to pasture."

"Never!"

"Easy for you to say now, but the antidote you marry will undoubtedly be jealous of your beautiful stepmama."

Danforth flung a light wig at his brother, which

the other skillfully dodged. "Antidote? Antidote? Why, you widgeon, any girl I choose will make you drool with envy."

"Touché." His brother was suddenly serious again. "A title and a fortune do rather appeal to the fair sex, I've noticed."

"Ah, yes. It is an indisputable fact of life. And speaking of which, tell me, Larry, if the subject's not too touchy, does the fact that Regina will most likely be at Stonebridge Park for Christmas have anything to say to your sudden reluctance to be parted from Audrey?"

"Naturally." Larry grimaced as he extracted a cheroot from his pocket. "It has everything to say to it, big brother."

"Then, Larry, you're a fool. And a damned one at that."

Chapter Two

"CHRISTMAS AT STONEBRIDGE? ABSOLUTELY NOT. I can't think of anything more dismal. You must have maggots in your head, Mama, even to suggest it."

Miss Regina Fielding stared at her mother over the top of the novel she was holding. She had moved her library chair next to the window of the book-lined room in order to receive the maximum of dim December light. But in point of fact she had spent more time gazing at the view than at the page. The barren rosebushes and brown grass of Bath's Royal Crescent had done little to lift a mood dangerously close to blue-deviled. Nor did her mother's announcement raise her spirits.

Miss Fielding was considered by most to be a diamond of the first water. Her few detractors, mothers of rivals for the most part, claimed that her nose was a bit too retroussé for true beauty. But that criticism seemed niggling when matched against raven hair, violet eyes, heart-shaped face, and flawless complexion. Even her present petulant expression could not spoil the effect.

In her first Season she had been the most sought-after of all the debutantes. But to her mother's horror she had dismissed even the most eligible of her suitors. It was beginning to be whispered that at twenty-two she was dangerously close to being left upon the shelf. Then, to her mother's ill-concealed delight, she had accepted the proposal of that long-elusive, extremely wealthy bachelor, Lord Elliott.

At the moment, though, her widowed mother was less than pleased with Regina. "I do not care for your tone, Regina. Not to mention your lack of respect in addressing me."

Mrs. Fielding, displeased, was accustomed to driving tweenies to tears and reducing footmen to quivering jellies. She had no such effect on her daughter.

Regina merely shut her book with a martyred sigh. "Well, what exactly did you expect from me? One does not jump up and down with glee at the prospect of burying oneself in Warwickshire for Christmas."

"One expects a bit of sensibility. Your grandfather is on his deathbed, Regina." Mrs. Fielding raised her starchiness a few more notches.

She was an imposing woman at any time. Tall, with classic features (her nose would not have dared be retroussé), she was of a type usually referred to as handsome. The only physical trait that she and her daughter had ever had in common was the color of their hair. But since Mrs. Fielding's locks were beginning to streak with gray, even that commonality was deserting them.

"Grandpapa dying? I seriously doubt it. If the old

horror wants to see us, I'll bet a monkey he has some ulterior motive." Despite herself, Regina was beginning to show some interest. "What exactly did he say?"

"*He* did not say anything." Mrs. Fielding drew up a chair from its post by the library table and ceased to loom over her offspring. "Not directly, that is. The invitation came from Anne." Mrs. Fielding could not suppress a slight sniff as she pronounced her distant cousin's name. "She simply wrote that Papa asked her to say that since it was undoubtedly his last Christmas, he wished to have his family gathered around him."

"*All* his family?" Regina's curiosity was definitely getting the better of her. "You don't suppose that he really means *all* his children?"

"I most certainly do not. Dismiss that notion. It is unthinkable.

"Anne goes on to say that she is also writing Audrey, of course. I doubt she will come, however. You know what a social butterfly my sister is." Mrs. Fielding's voice dripped disapproval. "She was never one to rusticate."

"She certainly won't come unless she is convinced that Grandfather is dying. And I collect you would do well to question his quack before we go haring off to spend a miserable Christmas at Stonebridge."

"I shall do no such thing. The important point is, Papa wants us there. And if Audrey has half a brain, she, too, will obey his summons. For I am of the opinion that he is putting us to the test. Deathbed or no deathbed, I vow he is thinking of altering his will. And as his only grandchild you of all people should be moved to see to your interests."

"Why?"

Mrs. Fielding could not believe her ears.

"Why? You ask *why*?"

"That was the question."

"Because, my naïve daughter, it would be just like your grandfather to cut us all out and leave everything to Anne Welbourne. Think on that for a moment."

Miss Fielding appeared to do so.

"I am sorry, Mama," she finally pronounced, "but I fail to be properly horrified at the prospect. Wasn't that the whole idea of my come-out, that I should capture a nabob for myself and be spared that kind of anxiety? Lord Elliott has far more brass than I shall ever be able to spend. So as far as I am concerned, Grandfather can dispose of his fortune any way he chooses."

"Regina!" Mrs. Fielding seemed close to apoplexy. "How can you speak so!"

"I just explained that. And if you think I have no regard for your interests—or for Aunt Audrey's, come to that—well, it appears to me that both of you are also most comfortably fixed."

"I was referring to the vulgarity of your speech and not to its content," her mother retorted. "Though as for the latter, if you cannot see the impropriety—no, not *impropriety*, the *disgrace* of having my father cut out his children and leave his fortune to a mere connection, well, then, I can only pity Lord Elliott and bemoan the fact that I failed to instill the proper family values in my daughter."

"I thought my values were in fine fig." Regina hid a smile. "I felt almost noble in wishing my cousin Anne so well. After all, the poor thing deserves something for putting up with that old curmudgeon all these years."

"I quite agree that she deserves *something*. What she does not deserve is my father's entire fortune. And I plan to make it my business to see that he does not do the unthinkable in his dotage. So we will go to Stonebridge. Resign yourself to that."

Miss Fielding knew when she was beaten. "Yes, Mama," she said with a sigh.

"And no need to make a Cheltenham tragedy of the business. We are to invite Lord Elliott as well."

"Elliott at Stonebridge Park for Christmas? Surely you must be funning."

"Nothing of the sort. Papa is most desirous of meeting him. And it is fitting that he do so."

"Christmas at Stonebridge with Grandfather—dying or not. Good heavens, Mama," she said, giggling, "Elliott is bound to cry off."

"Nonsense. It will be a very good thing for you and Lord Elliott to spend time together away from all the hurly-burly of the social scene. It will give you a chance to become well acquainted."

"Don't we have the rest of our lives for that?"

Mrs. Fielding picked up on her daughter's tone. "Sometimes, Regina," she snapped, "I get the impression that you do not know how fortunate you are to have fixed Lord Elliott's interest."

"Oh, but I do know, Mama. You have told me so often enough."

"There is not an unwed girl in England who would not gladly take your place. Lord Elliott has every characteristic desirable in a husband: wealth, position, good looks, amiability."

"You left out 'maturity,' Mama. It is usually high on your list of virtues."

"As it should be. It is all to the good for a husband to be older than his wife. And there is no need to make him out a graybeard. Lord Elliott is not yet forty.

"Come, Regina." Mrs. Fielding's look softened. "It is perfectly natural for a young lady to be apprehensive about her marriage. After all, you are stepping off into the unknown."

Not as unknown as you imagine, Mama. Regina did not speak the words aloud. Her mother would have been shocked to discover just how much about the expectations of the wedding night the sheltered young ladies at her exclusive boarding school had contrived to learn.

"Your Lord Elliott is the perfect gentleman," Mrs. Fielding was saying. "You can rest assured that he will be all sensibility when it comes to . . . certain matters between a husband and a wife."

"Really, Mama," Regina protested, "you do not have to keep on praising Elliott to the skies. I assure you that I am quite as aware of his sterling qualities as you are. I quite agree that he is superior to all my other suitors. And I like him prodigiously. Now are you satisfied?"

"I would be if you would show a bit more enthusiasm for the match. A certain amount of reserve is desirable in a young lady, Regina. But now that you and Elliott are betrothed, I do not think it necessary to be so . . . so . . . *distant.* For I am convinced that your seeming indifference troubles his lordship."

"I am not indifferent." Regina appeared stung. "I am most appreciative of my good fortune. It is just that . . ."

"Yes?" Mrs. Fielding prodded.

"I am not in love with him, Mama."

Regina's words were almost inaudible, but her mother heard them.

"Pshaw! If that is what is troubling you, put it out of your mind. Being in love has little to say to a successful marriage. Believe me, it is far more important to like one's husband 'prodigiously,' as you put it."

"You *are* a cynic."

"Nothing of the sort. I am simply versed in the ways of the world. Whereas I suspect that you, Regina, have been exposed to those dreadful romantic novels that circulate amongst impressionable schoolgirls. At least I trust that is what accounts for your megrims." She suddenly looked alarmed. "For you surely have more intelligence than to be still sighing over Audrey's stepson."

Regina's eyes snapped. "I can assure you, Mama, that Captain Hunt"—her lip curled at the name—"has nothing to say in this matter."

"Good. I am pleased to hear that you have outgrown your mooncalf infatuation. For I can assure *you* that there is no comparison between that here-and-thereian and Lord Elliott."

"None whatsoever."

If Regina's voiced avowal possessed a slightly hollow ring, neither lady seemed aware of it.

Chapter
Three

THE SCENE IN LORD HUNT'S BREAKFAST ROOM BORE A marked resemblance to the action that had taken place there two days previously. Lady Hunt was reading, and then rereading, a letter while her twin stepsons watched intently.

"Bad news?" Lawrence asked.

"Is your father worse?" Danforth prodded.

Audrey's eyes remained on the paper. "No. No. I'm just puzzled, that's all. It's from Judith. And I'm trying to read between the lines."

Lawrence, who had risen to go to the sideboard for a third helping of sirloin, squinted over her shoulder. "That would seem to be a problem," he commented. "She has crossed the damned thing."

It was true that Mrs. Fielding had confined her outpourings to a single sheet but had written upon it both horizontally and vertically. The intent was to save her sister extra postage.

"That is not what I meant, Peagoose. I can decipher her writing well enough. It is the meaning that eludes me. She spends the west to east part of the page telling me how important family solidarity is and how it behooves the two of us to go to Stonebridge and make sure that Certain People—capitalized and underlined—not take advantage of Papa in his present state."

"And what exactly is that supposed to mean?" Lawrence had returned to his place and was plying his knife and fork.

"I imagine that Judith thinks Anne is about to charm Papa into leaving her his fortune."

"Oh, really?" Danforth looked interested. "Would she do that? She did not strike me as the type."

"Nooo," Audrey replied thoughtfully. "I do not believe for a minute that Anne would try to exert any kind of influence. But still . . . I would not put it past Papa to cut his daughters off. After all, it is not as if he has not—" She bit off the observation. The twins exchanged covert glances.

"But then," Audrey continued, "after all that emphasis, west and east, upon proper family feeling, she stresses, north and south, that under no circumstances should I bring the two of you along."

"Really?" Two pairs of eyebrows shot upward.

"Taken against us, has she?" Lawrence inquired.

"What do you mean, *us*? You're the one she never liked above half."

"Well, I must say I think she has a nerve!" Two spots glowed in Audrey's cheeks. "Telling me that you two are not truly part of the family. Fustian! You are certainly more family than is Lord Elliott."

"Lord Elliott is going to Stonebridge?" Lawrence had stopped chewing.

"So Judith says."

"For Christmas?"

"Yes."

"Then that must mean that Regina will be there."

"No, Nodcock," his brother jeered. "Elliott is going in order to be near her mother."

"And Mrs. Fielding has written that you should leave your charming stepsons at home, has she?" Lawrence's face broke into a grin. "Well, well, well. I don't know about you, brother, but wild horses could not keep me away now."

That evening the twins, clad merely in small-clothes, stood over the washbasin in their common dressing room shaving and vying for space in the looking glass. Their evening clothes were laid out for a duty call at Almack's. That done, they would go on to a night of cards at White's Club for Gentlemen. Their valet stood by with a look of disapproval on his face. He would have much preferred to do the shaving.

"I say, brother"—Lawrence ran the straight razor skillfully down his taut jaw line—"just what do you make of the fact that the old battle-ax doesn't want us?"

"Which old battle-ax?"

"Mrs. Fielding, as you dashed well know."

"Isn't that obvious?" The valet winced as Danforth flipped whiskered lather off his razor, missed the basin, and splattered the washstand. "She doesn't wish to have you messing up her well-laid plans."

"Oh?" Lawrence looked hopeful. "Any chance of that, do you think?"

"Not a prayer."

The other grimaced. "By George, you always were the one for plain speaking."

"I was forced into the role early. You always were the one with your head in the clouds. And just in case you are still weaving fancies, let me remind you. The notice has appeared in the *Gazette*. Miss Fielding and Lord Elliott are well and truly betrothed."

"Ah, yes. But not, dear brother, well and truly wed. As Mama Fielding seems to realize, there's many a slip 'twix the cup and the lip."

"True. And you're the one most likely to take a fall. It may not have occurred to you, my charming relative, but Mrs. Fielding's chief reason for arranging your absence is not that you will come between the plighted couple but in the interests of Yuletide harmony. It behooves me to point out that Regina is, to put it mildly, quite out of charity with you. Her nostrils tend to flare at the mention of your name. Why, she can barely do the civil when we happen to meet."

"That seems hard."

"Oh, I agree. For God knows, my only crime is being your twin."

"I'm not referring to her treatment of you, stupid. I am saying that she has no real cause to hate me."

"Hmmm." Danforth accepted the towel the valet proffered and dried his face. "Some might consider being jilted due cause for becoming miffed."

"Damn, this thing is hot!" Lawrence reacted to his towel, then peered in the glass at his reddened face. "Trying to turn me into a lobster, Frederick?" He gave the valet a reproachful look.

"Sorry, sir."

"I deny it emphatically."

"Deny what?" Danforth was being helped into his cambric shirt.

"That I jilted Regina. Nothing of the sort."

"No? What else would you call joining the army and haring off to the Peninsula?"

"Patriotism?"

"Fustian."

"Well, not entirely, perhaps, but it certainly played a part. Mostly, I collect, I did not wish to miss out on the show of a lifetime."

"Obviously. But it certainly gave the gorgeous Miss Fielding's pride a tumble when you chose adventure over her. She was in love with you, you know."

"And I was in love with her. Still am, if it comes to that. I simply wasn't ready to be leg-shackled. Have to admit, though, that my attitude's undergone a sea change."

"So has hers," his twin said dryly.

"Loves the fellow, does she?"

"How would I know? The point is, my lad, that she is definitely going to marry him."

"And what's he like—besides old? To my knowledge I have never met his lordship."

"Well, in the first place he ain't all that old. More in the prime of life, you could say. Got all his hair and teeth. Good physique. All in all, a nice-looking cove."

"Plus possessing a fortune that would shame Midas. And a title." Lawrence groaned. "Well, it will be a challenge."

"It will be a rout. Don't be a fool, Larry." There was real concern on Danforth's face. "Let's take Mrs. Fielding's advice and stay in town for Christmas."

"And disappoint Sir Jervis? Never. Besides, even if I can't win Regina back, I should at least like to explain myself. For I certainly did not jilt her. The thing was, I couldn't declare myself before I left. There was always the possibility I wouldn't make it back. Or worse, come back an invalid. Wouldn't have been at all the thing to tie her down."

His brother looked at the ugly scar on Lawrence's

chest, perilously near the heart, and winced. "It almost happened."

"Well, yes." Lawrence fingered the wound. "I was lucky at that."

"Pity it doesn't show. Ladies do go for war heroes."

"Hmmm, that's so." Lawrence touched his cheekbone. "A saber nicked me here. Do you think it will rate a bit of sympathy?"

"Not a chance. Looks more like you cut yourself shaving. Of course, you could always wear your medals. May look a bit ostentatious on your dress coat at a country dinner; still, all is fair in love—"

"By Jove," Lawrence interrupted, snapping his fingers. "That's it. You've hit on a capital idea."

"To sport your medals at Stonebridge? Come now. You wouldn't. You must know that I was only funning."

"No, you ninnyhammer, not the medals. That other thing you mentioned. The war wounds. Pity is a powerful weapon. That's it. I'll work on Miss Regina Fielding's sympathy."

"Oh, dear God." His lordship groaned. "Come on. We're late."

The valet stepped back to inspect his charges. Their dark blue coats fitted admirably across their shoulders. Their white satin knee breeches hugged their thighs, and their equally white stockings showed off muscular calves to best advantage. Their shirt points were not absurdly high or unfashionably low, and their cravats were starched and tied to a perfection. Silver watch fobs gleamed and a pair of silver-handled quizzing glasses hung at the ready. Both young gentlemen wore their locks swept forward in a modish Brutus style. The valet frowned, then made a minute adjustment to his lordship's arrangement. Frederick was determined to be needed.

At last, pronouncing all to be perfection, he opened the dressing-room door and dismissed his charges for a night on the town.

Chapter Four

IT HAD BEEN DECIDED THAT LADY HUNT WOULD MAKE the journey to Stonebridge Park alone and that the twins would travel there a bit later on horseback. The arrangement had suited all three parties. The brothers hated the confinement of the family carriage and Audrey needed private time to think.

But by journey's end this mental exercise had done little more than bring on the headache. Audrey had examined the coil she was in from every angle and could find no solution.

She would not, could not, throw herself upon Danforth's mercy. While settling her debts would not ruin him, it would certainly force him to practice stringent economies and at a time when he had hoped to purchase a property for his brother. The financial consequence of her folly did not bear thinking about, but even worse was the prospect of falling from grace in her stepsons' eyes.

For she could not have loved the boys more had they been her own children—or, more logically, her own brothers. And she was well aware that their regard for her bordered on idolatry. To lose their esteem was a prospect she could not bear to face.

And from such a cause! She had spent her life trying to avoid so much as a taint of the family weakness. And to have been gulled into folly like a veritable flat, a green 'un! No, she could not bear to contemplate the—disappointment? pity? scorn?— her stepsons would feel. Debtors' prison would be preferable. Not that Danforth would allow things to come to that. He would put his own pockets to let first. Audrey groaned aloud as the carriage turned into the gates of Stonebridge Park. She had gone full circle in her mind and was back where she had started.

She sat up from her reclining position, smoothed out the skirts of her ermine-trimmed pelisse, and clapped her lutestring bonnet back upon her head. She did not bother to look out at the frosted vista as her crested carriage covered the final mile of parkland that led to her ancestral home. She felt no nostalgia for the place. Truth to tell, during most of her childhood she had been eager to grow up and see the last of it. Lord Hunt had seemed a knight in shining armor when he had offered for her. Audrey was made uncomfortable by the thought that his lordship might have represented the ideal father. She quickly dismissed it. But clearly Sir Jervis had been no paragon in that respect.

Not that the baronet had been cruel in any way. "Indifferent" would have described him best. He had clearly preferred his horses and his dogs to his children. And to his wife, when it came to that. Especially his wife. Audrey quickly cut off that train of thought. For this, she realized, was where the real pain lay.

They rounded the last curve and the hall loomed up before her. It was an enormous edifice, imposing more than pleasing. The architecture was as jumbled as her thoughts had been. One wing was very ancient, with stone-shafted, diamond-paned windows and walls that were overrun with ivy. The rest of the house reflected the French taste, having been added by an ancestor who had been chased to the Continent during the revolution and had returned home with the Restoration.

At the sight of the ancestral pile, Audrey felt her spirits sink even lower. How could she have pinned her hopes upon this visit when nothing good had ever come out of Stonebridge as far as she was concerned? Now the thought of pleading with her father to advance any sum he might plan to leave her in his will seemed totally insane.

Of course, if it were true that he was dying . . . Audrey quickly dismissed such an unworthy thought. She did not believe for a minute that Sir Jervis was on his deathbed. It was far more probable that Judith had it right: He wished to get his family together to gleefully inform them that he was leaving everything to Anne—or to his hounds—or to anything except his daughters. Disinheriting was no doubt habit forming. And their father had, most likely, become an addict.

Well, so be it, Audrey decided as the carriage swung around the horseshoe-shaped drive and halted before the main entrance to the house. Groveling was not in her nature. And this was Christmas. And the family was gathering. So what if her family was not the stuff of sentimentalists, she would still try to get through the holiday with the best grace possible. She would eat, drink, and do her utmost to be merry. For tomorrow—well, a pox upon tomorrow. Lady Hunt, aided by her father's footman, descended from her coach.

"Why, Anne, how grown up and pretty you are" was her spontaneous reaction to the young woman who, smiling shyly, came out to greet her.

It was easy to see why Judith feared Miss Welbourne. She was quietly attractive, with light brown hair, a small, neat figure, and an oval face made interesting by large, intelligent gray eyes. Obviously, she could be a soothing presence for a cranky, aged invalid. Still, Audrey saw no suggestion of the schemer in the steady gaze and open countenance.

"I dislike to rush your ladyship," Anne was saying as she ushered her inside, "but there is little time to dress for dinner." She laughed apologetically. "Even though Sir Jervis will have his own meal served, as usual, in his bedchamber, he insists that the rest of us keep country hours."

"How is my father?" Audrey hurried behind her hostess through the great hall and up the heavy wooden staircase. She glanced around her as she went. Little had changed. The hall was as gloomy as ever with its dark paneling presided over by an assortment of deer, elk, and boar heads, ancient ancestors of the animals that inhabited the park today. The only bright spot in the hall was a suit of burnished armor.

Anne seemed to choose her words carefully. "It is difficult to know. Dr. Ward thinks that he is as well as a man suffering from the usual infirmities of age can be. But Sir Jervis seems convinced that his days are numbered."

"I know." His daughter sighed. Whether from sympathy or vexation, neither woman was sure. "His last Christmas and all that."

Anne opened the door to a well-remembered bed-chamber, then left her ladyship to the ministrations of an abigail. Audrey hurriedly changed into a pale green gros de Naples dinner dress and entered the withdrawing room on the stroke of five.

This room also had changed little, she noted. Except that the deep red flocked wallcovering was more faded, and if she did not mistake the matter, the brocade window hangings were carefully draped to conceal time's tatters. The furnishings, in the French fashion, were still the same, only older, shabbier.

"Ah, Audrey, at last."

Mrs. Fielding, who would have been *de rigueur* at a London evening party in her lace over purple satin gown and her satin toque, crossed the room to give her sister a formal peck on the cheek. "You certainly seem no worse for your journey. A few tired lines about the eyes, perhaps. But at our ages that is to be expected."

Audrey bit back the retort that Judith was nine years her senior and turned to embrace her niece. "How lovely to see you again, my dear. In spite of the fact that you make me feel an ancient dowd."

She smiled affectionately at the young woman while at the same time assessing her. Regina was even more lovely than she remembered. Her British net over white satin gown was simple yet had cost a small fortune, Audrey surmised. Its only trim, a violet satin ribbon circling just beneath her breasts in the Empire fashion, enhanced the color of her striking eyes. She was, indeed, her aunt concluded, a nonpareil. Still, there had been a certain glow, as she recalled, that now seemed missing. But perhaps she was only romanticizing. Danforth always accused her of possessing too much imagination.

"Fustian," Regina was saying. "No one could ever make you appear a dowd. Come and meet my fiancé."

She pulled her aunt affectionately by the hand across the room, where a distinguished-looking gentleman had risen from a wingback chair to await them. He was tall with thick sandy hair, just beginning to be flecked with gray, and light blue eyes that widened as the ladies approached. "My word! Is it little Audrey Brougham? I don't believe it!"

"Edwin?" Lady Hunt had stopped in her tracks with a look of amazement on her face. "Is it really you? Oh, my heavens! I feel such a fool. I never made the connection."

Regina was looking from one to the other. "Shall I conclude that you two are already acquainted?" she asked dryly.

"Indeed we are." Her fiancé had reached out to take both of Lady Hunt's outstretched hands and beam down at her. "I knew Audrey—Lady Hunt, I should say—when she was barely out of leading strings. She and my sister were in school together." He released her hands, suddenly self-conscious.

"Yes, indeed. Arabella and I were bosom bows. I spent a Christmas at your house, remember? But you were plain Edwin Shelley then. I had no idea that you were heir to a title."

Mrs. Fielding joined them, appearing slightly annoyed by the intimacy. "It is a small world, is it not? I had no idea either that you two were acquainted. Though come to think on it, I do rather recall Arabella Shelley. She is Lady Marshall now, is she not? Her husband is a diplomat if I am not mistaken."

"He is, indeed. They are posted in India at the present."

"Really?" Audrey exclaimed. "How exciting for her. I do regret not having kept in touch. I cannot believe that my own niece is betrothed to an old friend and I had no notion of it."

"That is quite understandable," he said with a smile. "I was about to explain that I had never expected to inherit. But both my late uncle and his son died without issue and so . . ."

"I see. Now, may I offer my belated congratulations upon your betrothal? I admit to no prejudice when I say that you are a most fortunate fellow."

"Oh, I quite agree." He looked fondly at his fiancée before turning back eagerly to inquire of Lady Hunt, "And what of you, Audrey—your ladyship, I mean to say. What is your life like?"

Mrs. Fielding had had quite enough of the *tête-à-tête*. "Oh, Lady Hunt's life is full, indeed. Though unfortunately widowed like myself, she has two grown sons to occupy her time."

She was pleased at his lordship's astounded look. "Twins, as a matter of fact," she added as a *coup de grâce*.

"Stepsons, to be precise," Regina clarified.

"Oh, I see." Lord Elliott looked relieved. "I hardly believed it possible."

Judith turned toward her sister with a counterfeit smile. "And how are the young Corinthians? Caught up in the round of holiday parties, I collect. Bachelors are always in great demand, but particularly at this time of year. It is small wonder you could not force them from the metropolis."

"Oh, but I have. That is to say, there was no need to force them. For when Danforth and Lawrence received Papa's particular invitation, there was never the slightest doubt as to where they would spend their Christmas."

Mrs. Fielding's face had turned to stone. "How very considerate."

Her daughter, though, was not so skilled at hiding her emotions. Regina had gone quite pale and her voice shook slightly. "Are you serious, Aunt Audrey? Surely the twins would not wish to spend Christmas here. Why, Lawrence is only just back. How can he tear himself away from London?"

"Larry is not the care-for-nothing that he seems, m'dear," Lady Hunt said gently. "Underneath his devil-may-care façade, he is actually sentimental. So given the precarious state of his stepgrandfather's health, he really had no choice."

"Humph!"

This time Mrs. Fielding did not bother to hide her feelings. Lord Elliott looked at her curiously. Perhaps aware of the effect of her reaction, she rallied to ask politely, "And when might we expect the young gentlemen?"

"Oh, any time." Audrey glanced at the bracket clock upon the mantel. "I should have thought by now." She turned to Lord Elliott to explain. "My sons hate traveling by carriage, so they are coming on horseback. I cannot think what could have delayed them."

"Oh, they most likely have stopped at some inn for hot drinks," Elliott reassured her.

"Yes, it is bitter cold." Audrey eagerly accepted the explanation. "That is most likely."

She was interrupted by Anne Welbourne's hurried entrance. "I do beg pardon for leaving you on your own," she said breathlessly.

"No need to apologize. This is, after all, our home."

Mrs. Fielding's pointed set-down caused Anne's color to heighten just a bit, but her voice was calm. "Sir Jervis does not feel up to joining us. Nor in-

deed to seeing any of you until tomorrow. But"—
she smiled faintly—"he still required minute de-
tails of your separate arrivals. And I fear the delay
has put Cook upon her ear. Something to do with
the saddle of mutton, I collect. So," Anne concluded,
"shall we adjourn to the dining chamber before she
gives her notice?"

It had always irked Mrs. Fielding that her titled
younger sister had precedence over her. And al-
though in a family gathering no one else among
them—Lady Hunt, least of all—would have refined
upon such social niceties, she pointedly stepped
aside to allow her sister to lead the way. The procession had barely begun, however, when they were
halted by a lively commotion in the hall.

"Oh, that must be the twins now!" Audrey exclaimed.

"Splendid. Shall I have them join us as they are?"
Anne did not wait for consent but hurried toward
the door.

It opened, however, before she could reach it.
With an involuntary gasp she halted in her tracks
as the brothers stepped inside.

"Oh, my soul!" Mrs. Fielding's exclamation did
not carry beyond her sister's ears.

And the Dowager Lady Hunt, equally stricken,
was not sure just which of them had uttered it.

All eyes were glued upon the brothers. Or, to be
more exact, they had swept across Lord Hunt, clad
in top boots and riding coat, his cheeks still rosy
from the chilling ride, to fasten on his twin.

Captain Lawrence Hunt was dressed in uniform,
the dashing scarlet coat, dazzling gold braid, and
sky-blue trousers of the Life Guards Regiment. He
now stood regarding the company while leaning
heavily upon a cane. From the moment of his entrance it had been apparent that his every step was

agony, which he manfully strove to hide. Worst of all, a black satin patch obscured one eye. But his dazzling smile, which he flashed around the room, was the epitome of courage, completely lacking in self-pity. "Happy Christmas, everyone," he said.

"Oh, dear God, no!" Miss Regina Fielding moaned softly just before she sank slowly to the floor.

Chapter
Five

AUDREY AROSE THE FOLLOWING MORNING DETER-mined to beard the lion in his den. After a sleepless night her resolve was so fixed that even the news, delivered in a sonorous voice by the ancient valet, that Sir Jervis was not up to seeing anyone did not deter her.

"Nonsense." She pushed the cracked door wide open and brushed past the protesting servant.

Audrey found her father propped up in his four-poster noisily consuming a bowl of porridge. Her "Good morning, Papa" was greeted by a glare from under bushy eyebrows, "Didn't Carter tell you I was not up to company?"

"Oh, yes. But I fail to see the point in leaving London and all the holiday gaiety to come to Stonebridge Park and never catch a glimpse of you. Your letter said you wished your family around you at Christmastime, remember?"

"It didn't say I wished them in me bedchamber. A dying man deserves his privacy, by God."

"Well, I must say, you look remarkably hale for a man with the grim reaper hovering." She pulled up a chair and sat down beside the bed, uninvited.

"And you look remarkably girlish for someone so long in the tooth. Mutton dressed as lamb, is it?" He assessed her stylish morning dress of rose-and-white-striped silk. "How old are you by now, Audrey? Pushing forty, is it?"

She refused to rise to his bait. "I am thirty-three."

"Well, can't say as you look it." There was a bit of pride in the grudging compliment. "You take after the Broughams in that respect. Now Judith is more like her mother's folk. The Woodens don't age half so well."

"My mother was a beautiful woman." In spite of all her resolve Audrey felt her anger and resentment begin to rise. "And remained so until the day she died."

"Yes, but she didn't live that long, now did she?" Sir Jervis polished off the last noisy spoonful of porridge and placed the bowl on the table beside him. "Who's to say what she would have turned into had she lived? Her mother was a regular old crone. Now Regina," he reflected, "is more like you than Judith. I expect she will wear well.

"And speaking of Regina"—he gave his daughter a sly look—"I understand she's taken to her bed."

"Yes. Judith fears she is coming down with the grippe. A day in bed should put her to rights, however."

"The grippe, is it?" The old man chuckled. "Cod's-wallop! I was told she swooned away when she saw that son of yours. Had no notion of the seriousness of his wounds. And when it comes to that, neither had I. Why did you not let me know he was crippled and had lost an eye?"

Audrey looked uncomfortable and hesitated. "Lawrence does not like to have it discussed," she said finally. "He tries not to refine too much upon his disabilities and does not wish others to do so."

"I see." The old man sounded almost approving. "Always was a plucky 'un. More so than that twin of his."

"That is untrue!" No one could ever criticize Lady Hunt's stepsons, as her close friends had discovered early on. "Danforth is every bit as brave as Larry. He is simply more reserved, that is all."

"Hmmm. Mayhap you're right. You know 'em better than I do. But I do know this much. Larry's the one the females were all wild about. Including me own granddaughter. And don't try to tell me anything different."

"I would not dream of contradicting you," his daughter said sweetly. "But that was years ago. Mooncalf business. Regina has long since got over it."

"She has, has she?" The old man chuckled wickedly. "Then why is she collapsing on me carpet? Tell me that, Miss Know Everything."

"You don't miss much, do you? No wonder you don't bother to stir from this bed. There is no need for it. You seem to have a regular spy operation going."

"Nothing of the sort. Servants always know everything about us. I just pay 'em handsomely enough so that they pass everything on to me."

"Even so, I trust that you are going to grace us with your presence at some point. Firsthand experience of your family might be better than hearsay."

"Take on the lot of you *en masse*?" He gave her an evil grin. "Me heart would never survive it. Why,

I'll have to take a double dose of me drops just to recover from this interview with you. Now get along with you, girl." He waved dismissively.

"But there is something I wish to discuss first, Papa."

"Not now." He had sunk back against his pillows and did indeed look quite drained of strength. "Can't you see I'm knocked up? Get on with you."

Audrey sighed and rose from her chair. "Rest well, Papa."

"Yes, yes." He waved her away impatiently.

But as she was opening the door he roused enough to call, "Tell me, Audrey, how is it you have never remarried? Hunt's been dead for donkey's years."

"I just never met anyone I cared to marry," she said evenly.

"Nor after growing up in this house did I value the institution very highly," she muttered once the door was safely closed behind her.

As she passed the library, Audrey happened to glance into the room and saw Lord Elliott, his hands behind his back, staring at the shelves, perusing titles.

"Why, Edwin," she said as she joined him, "don't tell me you have been left on your own." She suddenly looked embarrassed. "Oh, dear. I should not address you so familiarly. Childish habits die hard, I fear."

"Don't be daft. Of course you should call me by my given name." He looked very pleased to see her. "Not only are we old friends, we are about to become family. Dashed if I will call you Aunt Audrey, though. Come, sit down." He gestured toward the large fireplace, which was fronted by a grouping of sofas and chairs. "I am longing for a coze."

For a bit, as they recalled and laughed over the

pranks and escapades of her visits to his family's seat, the conversation stayed comfortably in the past. "I am flattered that you recall so much," she remarked as the reminiscences ran down. "You seemed so far above Arabella's and my touch in those days that I wonder you would even associate with us, let alone join so wholeheartedly in our foolery. But of course," she recalled, "there was little else for you to do during your school holidays."

"Believe me, it was no sacrifice to dance attendance on my sister's beautiful friend." He chuckled. "For I had a near-fatal schoolboy case of calf love."

Her eyes widened. "For me? I'll not believe it. I had no idea."

"Oh, I was far too shy to declare myself. But, trust me, I suffered." His smile was a bit rueful.

"Indeed? Well into the following week, I've no doubt," she teased. "Of course, I fully expect you to confess now that you fell in love with Regina because she reminded you of me. At least some people do say she looks like me, though I find that ridiculous. Our coloring is quite different."

"By George," he exclaimed, snapping his fingers. "You are probably right. Why did I never recognize that fact?" He stared a moment into the flames. "Yes, come to think on it," he mused, "there is a resemblance. She is truly lovely, is she not?"

"Good heavens. What a coil I'm in. Here I have just said we are thought to look alike, so I would appear to be fishing for compliments. But, yes, Regina is lovely. And I don't mind admitting that even were we the same age I would be quite cast in the shade. Oh, goodness, this is a dampening conversation. Let us change the subject."

"No, let us not. For age is the very thing I need to speak of." He was suddenly quite intense. "As you know, Audrey, I am much older than your niece. And this concerns me."

"Well, it should not. In the first place, you are not that much older."

"Fifteen years by my arithmetic."

"But that is all to the good. My husband was twenty years older than I. And ours was a most successful marriage."

"Indeed? And just how long has he been dead? Oh, I am sorry, Audrey. That was a tasteless remark meant to be facetious."

"No need to apologize. But I will assure you that my husband died of an accident and not old age. And I will also assure you that you are concerning yourself over nothing. I am firmly of the opinion that a marriage is the most successful when the husband is older and wiser than the wife."

"Thank you for the encouragement. Which I know is sincere. But may I speak plainly?"

"Of course."

"I could not help but notice Regina's reaction to your stepson's arrival. Well"—he grimaced—"that was certainly ill put. Who could have failed to notice her collapse? She was obviously distraught by Captain Hunt's appearance."

"That is understandable." The captain's stepmother struggled with her conscience. She could not bring herself to betray Larry. Nor could she lie for him. "Even though we had only been separated briefly," she equivocated, "I must confess that my initial reaction when Lawrence limped in last night was shock."

"I did ask for plain speaking, remember? So let me say bluntly that I do not believe for a moment that Regina was merely exhibiting the usual sort of pity one would feel for a maimed soldier. I am convinced there is more to it than that."

"Of course there is. She has known Larry all her life. They are cousins, for goodness' sake. Of course she was distraught. No one had warned her of his . . . disfigurement."

"Oh, come now, Audrey. Pray don't spar with me. They are *not* cousins. And I have heard rumors— well, more than rumors, actually. The gossipmongers have been at pains to let me know that she was once in love with him."

"Pshaw!" Audrey wondered if she sounded like Judith. She had never used that exclamation in her life. "Mooncalf business. Much the same, no doubt, as the *tendre* you said you had for me. That was all donkey's years ago. It is long over."

"You are sure? I do hope you are right. But somehow I cannot help but wonder if there is some connection between this sudden onslaught of the grippe and Captain Hunt's arrival. Regina seemed perfectly healthy up to that point."

"But the grippe is like that, is it not? Who knows when it will suddenly strike? Come now, Edwin. Since we are speaking plainly, allow me to say that you are letting your imagination run rampant."

"Perhaps." He sounded skeptical.

"Most definitely. You are turning a slight matter of an age difference into a Cheltenham tragedy of imagined obstacles."

"Well," he said, smiling his crooked smile once more, "I certainly desire to be convinced of that. For it would be difficult enough to compete with a handsome man so much my junior. But to compete with a younger, handsome, wounded war hero . . ." He shuddered. "My God, it doesn't bear thinking on."

Chapter Six

THE REMAINDER OF THE DAY SEEMED DEVOTED TO avoidance. Sir Jervis showed no signs of wishing to encounter any of the family he had gathered around him. Miss Fielding also kept to her bed, instructing the chambermaid to turn away her concerned fiancé for fear she was infectious. Her mother was not so easily put off. "You cannot skulk in your room until the New Year, you know," Mrs. Fielding scolded.

"Why not? Grandpapa seems to manage quite well."

"None of your impertinence. After the spectacle you made of yourself last night, you owe it to Elliott to behave normally now. We are all sorry for Captain Hunt's wounds, Regina. But you must not allow your fiancé to believe you refine too much upon them."

Regina recovered enough to sit up in bed and glare at her mother. "Too much? Too *much*! And just what is the proper concern for a lost eye, pray tell?" After which outburst she let loose a flood of tears and buried her face in her pillow.

Mrs. Fielding left her daughter's bedchamber to go in search of her sister. She had every intention of ringing a peal over Audrey for being so inconsiderate as to allow her stepsons to come to Stonebridge after she had particularly requested that they not do so.

She did not succeed in this mission for two reasons. For one, Lady Hunt had anticipated her reaction and was at some pains to avoid her. For another, Audrey had her own peal to ring. She was determined to corner Larry and see just what sort of havey-cavey game he was playing. And though it went against her grain to comply with her sister's wishes, she was seriously considering packing the young men off to London. But since her stepsons were also avoiding everyone by spending the day hunting, Audrey, like her sister, was finally forced to give up her mission and return to her bedchamber to change for dinner.

So what with one thing and another, all of the houseguests did not come together until dinner was served.

That meal was a strained affair. Miss Welbourne, in her uncomfortable role of hostess, did her best to stimulate conversation. She was aided in this endeavor by the usually taciturn Lord Hunt. But the subject of the weather, focused on the probabilities of snow for Christmas, soon fizzled out to be followed merely by the sound of silver knives and forks contacting with fine bone china.

Regina, pale but lovely in white muslin, kept her slightly red-rimmed eyes fastened upon her plate. Captain Hunt covertly watched her with his uncovered eye while Lord Elliott and Mrs. Fielding, just as covertly, watched him watching her.

Audrey had also been observing her younger stepson, intent on composing the most scathing tongue-lashing possible to be delivered at the first private moment. How best to convey her disgust at the tasteless deception he was engaged in fully occupied her thoughts even when her eyes finally strayed from the object of her displeasure. Indeed she had been gazing across the table at her sister for some little time before what her eyes beheld registered within her brain. When the connection was at last made, Audrey drew in her breath with an audible gasp. "Judith!" she exclaimed indignantly. Everyone's attention focused upon Mrs. Fielding.

Perhaps with the intention of rising above her daughter's mopes, that lady had dressed for dinner with considerable care, wearing ostrich feathers in her hair and a gown of rather daring décolletage. The focal point of her costume was, however, the ornate diamond necklace that drew attention away from the overly exposed shoulders and bosom. Her sister's horrified eyes were now glued upon this adornment.

"You are wearing Mama's necklace," Audrey accused.

While everyone stared at the jewelry, Mrs. Fielding's color rose. "Why, yes," she said.

"But how did you come by it?" Her ladyship made no attempt to mask her indignation. "There was no will."

"Well, I certainly did not help myself to it, if that is what you are thinking." Mrs. Fielding obviously did not care for her sister's tone.

"You mean Papa gave it to you?"

"No, certainly not. This hardly seems the time to

discuss the matter, but if you must know, Mama gave it to me herself. Upon her deathbed. She was most desirous that I take it. She feared that—" With an effort Mrs. Fielding cut off an indiscretion. "She had her reasons," she finished lamely, "which certainly were no reflection on you."

"No? Well, it seems deuced odd that—"

A series of loud noises emanating from the great hall prevented the fascinated diners from learning just what seemed odd to her ladyship.

First the bell clanged long and insistently. Next the heavy door slammed several times. Feet were heard stamping noisily. Raised voices reverberated. Then a rackety climax came in a horrendous crash of metal upon flagstone. In accord the diners jumped up from their places and rushed as a body toward the source.

They froze in unison, confronted by the tableau in the hall.

A small boy, none too clean, with a shock of reddish hair, widened green eyes, and a profusion of freckles was staring down at the prone suit of armor at his feet. Its detached helmet was still clanging across the black-and-white-checked floor. A tall man wearing a five-caped greatcoat, a curly beaver, and an exasperated expression held the child firmly by the arm. He was absently shaking him back and forth in detached reproof.

"You little bastard." The tone was fond. "Couldn't wait for me to get me coat off, could you, to get up to your starts."

Audrey gasped and, all else forgotten, clutched her sister's arm. "Oh, my God, Judith," she whispered. "It's Chalgrove."

"Well, why the devil are you all standing there gaping like a pack of fools?"

In the commotion no one had noticed Sir Jervis, who had materialized upon the landing still wearing his nightshirt and nightcap with a candle in his hand.

"Get to bed the lot of you," he barked. "As for you, sir"—he glared down at the newcomer—"your presence here requires an explanation. Now." He turned to climb the remaining stairs, then had a second thought. "Johns!"

The butler appeared to be in shock. He returned to reality with an effort. "Yes, Sir Jervis?"

"Brandy. A lot of it. And be quick about it."

"Capital idea." The newcomer smiled as he shrugged, unassisted, out of his coat. "And I say, Johns, could you manage a bit of food? We didn't stop at the Rose and Briar. Didn't wish to rouse the house from bed, you know. So I am famished. Anything will do, actually. But ain't a fatted calf the custom in these cases?"

He laughed heartily at his own humor and looked expectantly at his audience for their appreciation. But when their only reaction was either shock or bewilderment, he shrugged philosophically and started toward the stairs.

"Oh." He suddenly recalled the presence of the child and turned around again. "My God, what next!" he roared. "Take that thing off, you little demon!"

While all attention had been fixed elsewhere, the lad had retrieved the helmet and placed it on his head. He was now struggling to raise the rusted visor.

Obediently he shifted his objective and tried to lift the heavy headpiece off his shoulders. It did not budge. Grunting with the effort, he strained harder. Then harder still.

"Oh, help! I can't! It's stuck! Help! Help! Help! Bloody murder! Help!"

The panicked voice echoed hollowly within the metal trap.

Chapter
Seven

"HERE. ALLOW ME." CAPTAIN HUNT, NEAREST THE child, went to the rescue. It was a testimony to the houseguests' shock that no one noticed when he failed to limp.

"Hang on a second," he said soothingly as the small boy tugged frantically and futilely at the metal that imprisoned him and then began to howl. The sound, emerging as it did from the warlike helmet, was particularly unnerving.

"Stop that caterwauling!" the man on the stairs snapped. And to everyone's amazement it stopped. Only the merest muffled sniffles were heard.

In the meantime Larry had also been frustrated in his attempts to remove the helmet in the normal way and was now exploring underneath it with his hand. "Ouch!" he yelped suddenly. "The little devil bit me!"

"Behave yourself, Fitz," the boy's father commanded.

"He poked me eye!" came back an echoing wail.

"Ah, here's the problem," Larry breathed. "There's a leather strap here that's gotten tangled in his scarf. Hold still a bit. Ah . . . That should do it." And he gently lifted the helmet to reveal a much-relieved tear-streaked face. "Are you all right now?" he asked solicitously.

The little boy stared up at him solemnly before answering. "Better than you, I'll bet a monkey. Somebody must of really given your eye a poke. Can I see it?"

"Fitz! That will do! Told you to be on your good behavior, didn't I?" The man on the stairs suddenly grinned at the company. "Fact of the matter, this *is* his good behavior.

"Well, I'd best see what the old tyrant wants before he flies off into the boughs. Will someone feed me boy?" He ran cheerfully on up the staircase.

Sir Jervis had climbed back into bed and was propped up against the headboard. The high four-poster, occupying as it did the center of the room, gave him, he felt, the best advantage for the upcoming interview. He was not so sure, however, when the young man was actually standing beside it.

"For God's sake, Chalgrove, sit. Can't abide you looming over me that way."

He continued to glare as his son obediently dragged an armchair across the room and plopped down in it. "By God, you must have grown since you left here. Don't recall you being such a tall 'un."

"Either that or you've shrunk a bit," the other said with a grin. "Happens in old age they tell me."

"Just as impudent as ever, I see," Sir Jervis growled. "Well, now, get on with it."

"On with what?" The visitor looked puzzled.

"On with your explanation, Lobcock. You can't just waltz in here cool as you please after donkey's years. I threw you out, remember? Told you never to darken me door again."

"Of course I remember. Not likely to forget a thing like that. You didn't half create a scene." He shuddered at the memory.

"Then what the devil are you doing here?"

Chalgrove Brougham was looking at his father as if the old man had taken sudden leave of his senses. "You invited me. For Christmas. Insisted upon it."

"I did no such thing."

"I beg pardon, but you did. Don't have the letter with me, actually. Didn't expect to have to produce it at the door like some blasted card of invitation. But it was a most civil composition. A lot in it, as I recall, about a man needing his family around him at Christmas. At his *last* Christmas, come to think on it. Yes, by George, that's how you put it. Made it sound obligatory, don't you know. Though now I'm wondering if you weren't doing it up a bit too brown. You don't look to me like a cove that's about to pop off at any minute. But be that as it may, you did stress Christmas and family and all that sort of thing. And there was even a bit about letting bygones be bygones. So"—he stretched out his arms in an expansive gesture—"here I am.

"Oh, good. Here's me supper. And your brandy."

After the servant had deposited the brandy on the bedside table plus a cold collation of ham, turkey, cheese, and fruit and had then closed the door behind him, Chalgrove attacked the food like a man without a thought in the world other than satisfying his hunger pangs. His father, an enigmatic expression on his face, watched him masticate for a bit and then observed, "Must've been Anne. That's the only explanation."

"Beg pardon?"

It was obvious that Chalgrove had lost the thread of the previous conversation.

"Anne, you lobcock. She must have written the letter you got."

"That so?" Chalgrove stuffed an enormous forkful into his mouth and observed thickly, "Capital ham, this. Had forgot how good the home-cured stuff can be. But as you were saying, come to think on it, someone else did write the thing—but at your behest, I gathered. Who the devil is Anne, by the by? And why the deuce should she be writing me?"

"She's me ward. And companion."

"Oh, I see."

"You do nothing of the kind." His father glared. "And I'd thank you to pull your mind up out of the gutter. She's me second cousin Lizzy's child. Been with me ever since she was orphaned."

"Indeed? Is she that nonpareil I saw in the hall? The one with the violet-colored eyes?"

"No. That's your sister Judith's chit."

"Judith produced that? I'll not believe it! Now if she had belonged to Audrey—"

"Will you forget about Regina? She has nothing to say in the matter."

"But Anne does." Chalgrove nodded like a bright pupil who had answered a poser. "Let's see. She must have been the mousy one."

"Nothing of the sort," the old man bridled. "She is a very pretty girl."

"Oh, really? Well, perhaps had she not been standing next to the nonpareil—"

"The point is"—exasperation was about to get the upper hand—"Anne must have written you that letter along with the other family invitations."

"Then you knew nothing about it?"

"That's right."

"So I am not invited. Seems I have crashed the family party. Oh, well, then Fitz and I will clear out first thing tomorrow morning."

"Now wait a bit. No need to go off half cocked. If Anne thought it was the thing to ask you—well, mayhap she has the right of it. Christmas is not the time to harbor ill will."

Chalgrove brightened. "You are right as usual, sir. 'Peace on Earth' and all that sort of thing. Shall we stay on then?"

"So it's *we* now, is it? Hadn't bargained on you having a brat with you. Did you actually marry that doxy you ran off with?"

"Marry Flossie? Good God, no! You must take me for a lobcock."

There was a pause. "You'd best explain, then, about the lad."

"Fitz?" The other groaned. "I never try to explain the unexplainable. But he is definitely my son, if that is what you wish to know."

"Well, it was demmed decent of you to take him in charge." The old man gave his son a look of grudging approval.

"Demmed right it was. Regular little limb of Satan. You can't know the half of it." Fitz's father sighed. "But you will learn, sir. I fear that you will learn."

Chapter Eight

FOR SOME TIME AFTER CHALGROVE'S DEPARTURE, THE Christmas guests stood huddled in the hall, apparently in a state of shock. They seemed reluctant to follow their host's command. Except for Regina, who suddenly awakened to the fact that Larry was standing close beside her. Her expression approached panic. "Grandpapa says we should go to bed." She gave her family a forced smile. "So I bid you all good night."

"I had hoped we could talk." Larry's voice was a mere whisper, for her ears alone. But evidently it missed its mark for she moved away to light one of the candles set out for them and hurried with it up the stairs.

Danforth nudged his twin. "I think I shall have a brandy first. How about you, brother?"

Larry seemed mesmerized as his eyes followed Regina. "What? Oh, a brandy. Yes, of course."

"Will you join us, Lord Elliott?" Danforth asked politely.

Elliott, too, had been watching Regina mount the stairs. But he quickly returned his attention to his surroundings. "Oh, I think not, thank you. I am rather tired. Bed and a book sound appealing." He remained where he was, however, as the twins, after a general good night, made their way back to the dining chamber. Mrs. Fielding excused herself, also claiming exhaustion.

Anne Welbourne looked uneasily at the little boy, who had been staring at each adult in turn. She seemed, by default, to be in charge of him. "I think you should be in bed, young man. But first your supper. Come with me and we'll see what Cook can do for you in the kitchen."

Audrey and Lord Elliott found themselves deserted. "Well, after this shock I, for one, do not expect to sleep ever again," she declared. "I propose to proceed to the drawing room and ring for tea as if this were a normal evening. Are you actually as exhausted as you claim or would you care to join me?"

"I should like to very much. My excuses must have sounded as false as they are. There is no appealing book."

"Of course I cannot guarantee the tea," she said over her shoulder as she led the way. "The servants' hall must be on its ear with excitement by now."

But tea was forthcoming, steaming and aromatic. And after they had settled themselves before the fire, they sipped it appreciatively. "Well"—Lord Elliott gave a dry chuckle—"it seems I am once again obliged to seek an explanation from you. What in blazes was that scene about that I just witnessed? Who exactly are these late-arriving guests? They certainly seemed to create a . . ." He hesitated.

"Panic?"

"I was about to settle on 'stir' rather than put it quite so baldly. But to be perfectly honest, for a minute there I did think my future mother-in-law was going to need some feathers burned beneath her nose."

Audrey laughed. "Poor Edwin. You must be thinking you are marrying into a nest of Bedlamites."

"Well, not entirely." He gave her a fond look. "But there do seem to be more currents swirling around me than I can deal with."

"Oh, Chalgrove is much more like a tidal wave than a current. He is my scrapegrace brother. Papa's youngest child. Whom he ordered—oh, around ten years ago, as I recall—out of this house, never to darken its door again. Nor was his name ever to be spoken in Stonebridge Park. He was disgraced and disinherited."

"Dear God! But why?" He reddened. "Pray forgive me. That is a most improper question. I have no right."

"Of course you have. You are about to marry into the family and need to be aware of all the skeletons in our closet. Oh, please don't look so horrified," she teased. "Really, there are not all that many more waiting to pounce. Chalgrove is by far the worst.

"And to answer your question, well, Chalgrove's story is sordid but not all that unusual. First, he was sent down from Oxford. But instead of coming home and facing our father, he went to London to sponge off his friends. While there he managed to run up enormous gaming debts. When his creditors closed in, he returned home and appealed to Papa to pay them. Papa refused to do so. Chalgrove then threatened to leave the country in company with the opera dancer he had been keeping during his London stay. He appeared to think he could black-mail our father into preserving the family's good name. He should have known better." She smiled wryly. "Papa merely blew the roof right off the hall and told Chalgrove to go to the devil and take his lightskirt with him.

"So now you know the shocking truth," she concluded.

"Regrettable more than shocking, I'd call it. For as you say, the tale is not all that unusual. Wild-oat sowing is epidemic with young gentlemen. The important thing is that now, after all these years, your brother has come back."

"Yes. And as for what that means—well, your guess is as good as mine."

"And the boy?"

"Oh, he has to be Chalgrove's by-blow. Looks just like him. At least as Chalgrove looked at the same age." She suddenly began to laugh.

"What is it?" He smiled.

"I was so thunderstruck by my brother's sudden appearance that at the time I failed to appreciate just how f-funny the child looked s-stuck in that helmet."

Her laughter was contagious. Captain Hunt, on his way to bed while his brother indulged in a sec-ond brandy, heard the sound and came to the door to investigate. He discovered Audrey and Elliott holding their sides and gasping for breath. It oc-curred to him that he had not seen Audrey laugh so since he'd come back. The two were far too con-vulsed to notice him standing there. He started to speak, then changed his mind and slipped quietly away.

As he climbed the stairs, candle aloft, Larry was so deep in thought that he quite forgot to limp. It was fortunate that the only person in his vicinity was far too preoccupied to notice.

Master Fitz, his hands upon his knees, was bent in half with one eye glued to a keyhole. A faint light was shining from underneath the bedchamber door. Larry was all too aware that this was the room occupied by Regina Fielding.

"Just what the devil do you think you're doing?" He reached down to jerk the lad upright by his collar.

"Yow!" The boy let out a howl.

"Hush, you little monster. Do you want to wake the world?"

The warning came too late. The door was jerked open to reveal Miss Fielding, wearing a ruffled white nightcap tied becomingly beneath her chin with pink ribbons and clutching a matching dressing gown around her. "What is going on?" Her eyes widened at the scene.

"I've caught a peeping tom."

The boy, held fast in the soldier's grasp, was squinting upward at his face. The word *peeping* worked on him like an actor's cue. "Hey, lemme peep under that patch, will you?"

The request brought on a horrified gasp from Miss Fielding and a good hard shake from Captain Hunt.

"Give you tuppence for just one peep."

"Oh, do be careful, you'll hurt him." The shaking had increased.

"Get along with you, you disgusting little scrub." Larry gave the lad a push in the direction of his bedchamber, then quickly stepped inside Regina's and closed the door behind him. This much accomplished, he whipped out a handkerchief and stuffed a corner of it into the keyhole.

"What do you think you are doing?" she demanded.

"Making sure the little monster doesn't repeat his tricks. You do realize, don't you, that he had one eye pressed to your keyhole when I caught him?"

"I meant, what do you think you are doing barging into my bedchamber? Get out immediately."

"Oh, no need to be alarmed, Gina. I've no wicked intentions. As a matter of fact"—he smiled a most pathetic smile—"I doubt I could live up to them even if I had. I just want the chance to talk to you. You've dodged me like a leper ever since I came here."

"We have nothing to talk about. And even if we had, we would not do it in here. And in the middle of the night. With me in my nightclothes. If Mama should catch us . . ." She shuddered at the thought.

"Mama?" His brows went up. "I would have thought you would be more concerned with Lord Elliott."

"Not a bit of it. *He* would accept my explanation that you barged in here against my will."

"How noble," he murmured. "But still, let's not give him too much credit." He limped slowly and painfully farther into the room. "I am, after all, a negligible rival."

Without thinking, she hurried to pull a chair toward him. He sank into it gratefully. "Thank you. Still can't stay on my feet too long, you know."

Tears welled up in her eyes as she stood over him. "Oh, Larry. I am so sorry."

He bravely waved away her pity.

"Speaking of Lord Elliott," he continued, "I should congratulate you on your betrothal."

Her chin went up. "One does not congratulate the bride-to-be. One wishes her happy."

"Oh, I do. I do. But at least allow me then to congratulate your mother. Lord Elliott appears to be everything she ever wished for you. Titled. Wealthy—"

"Don't forget handsome . . . charming . . . dependable."

"That, too. And of course ancient. Dull as well, most likely."

"He is not ancient." Her eyes flashed. "I admire maturity in a man. And as for dull, he certainly may be by your standards. But I prefer to think of him as dependable."

"You do appear inordinately fond of that particular word."

"I am. Its opposite is unfaithful."

"Well, thank you, Miss Fielding, for that lesson in vocabulary." He was forgetting to be pathetic and matched her fire with fire. "But if that barb was meant for me, it misses the mark by a mile. For I was never unfaithful to you."

"Oh, no? And just what would you call vowing your undying love, then sneaking off to join the army?"

"I would certainly not call it being unfaithful. Why, I never even looked at—that is to say, I never ever loved anyone but you."

"There are other kinds of infidelity, sir, besides skirt chasing. Which is not to say you weren't quite accomplished in that pursuit."

"I was not." Her words stung him. "Oh, very well, I'll admit to a dalliance or two. But nothing ever of a serious nature. Anyhow"—he recollected himself and sighed—"that is all water under the bridge. But as for 'sneaking off to join the army,' I did nothing of the kind. I wrote you, remember?"

"Oh, yes. You informed me in a letter of your decision. A letter." Her voice was bitter. "How cowardly."

"Yes, I was a coward. I admit it. For I knew that if I told you in person, then I would have wound up asking you to wait for me. Which my conscience said I must not do. But I never stopped thinking of you, Gina," he said huskily, rising with great difficulty. "They tell me that when I was in the hospital—delirious—that I kept murmuring your name. Over and over and over." He took a quick peek with his one eye to see how she was taking this. Her head was bowed down; tears were glistening on her cheeks.

"Gina," he repeated, moving nearer. She would not meet his eye. "Would you have waited, Gina?" he asked softly.

There was a long silence.

"Oh, well." He shrugged. "It is too late to speculate. But at least it is obvious now why I dared not risk it. I was afraid of returning home like this. Or worse. And"—his voice broke—"I wished to spare you that." He reached out and gently brushed her tears away with his fingers.

She was about to speak when they heard footsteps coming down the hall. Larry silently cursed their timing. They both ceased to breathe as the steps paused a moment by her chamber door and then moved on again.

"Oh, dear heavens," she whispered. "That was most likely Mama. It is a miracle she did not come in."

"I don't think so—that it was your mother, I mean," he whispered back. "Sounded a bit heavy for her. Though she does appear to have put on a stone or two since I last saw her. My guess is that it was Lord Elliott. Saw him having a comfortable coze with Audrey a bit ago." He paused a moment to gauge her reaction to this bit of news and was

62

satisfied when he got none. "It was a miracle that *he* did not come in."

She tossed her head. "Elliott would never do such an improper thing."

"He is farther over the hill than I thought then," he said with a grin.

"Nothing of the sort. He is a gentleman."

Larry bit back a retort. This would not do. They were bickering again. He needed to get back to where they had been when the footsteps interrupted them.

"You are right, of course." He gave a long, deep sigh. "I should not have said what I just did. You must forgive my jealousy. I am trying hard to conquer it. But it is difficult for someone who is only half a man not to be jealous of a whole one. Especially one who has you, Gina."

His eye had been fixed on his evening slippers, but now he gave a quick glance to see how his last speech had gone down. Apparently, very well, indeed.

"You must go, Larry. Please don't say any more." The words obviously cost the speaker considerable effort.

"I know," he breathed. "I, too, can play the gentleman. I only desired to wish you happy, Regina. And then do this."

Captain Lawrence Hunt, late of His Majesty's Life Guards, knew the value of a surprise attack. Before Miss Fielding had the slightest inkling of his intention, she found herself encircled by his arms, pressed against his chest, and wooed with intense passion by his lips.

Memory and desire played into his hands. Regina cooperated to his total satisfaction in a lengthy, practiced kiss. No alarm bells rang in her conscience when he untied the ribbons of her cap, then tossed it aside in order to entwine his fingers in her hair as the kiss continued. It was only when he tried to apply the same technique to her dressing gown that conscience (taking the form of a mental vision of her mother) got the upper hand.

"Oh, do stop it," she moaned, and wrenched herself free. "I am betrothed, remember?"

Oh, hell.

"Please go, Larry. And you must forget me."

He smiled a martyr's smile. "Very well, then. I will go. For your sweet sake. But as for forgetting you, you ask what is impossible."

His movement toward the door was painful to watch. It was plain that his physical infirmity had been worsened by a breaking heart. With an actor's instinct, he paused by the door to look behind him and give his beloved one last, brave smile. "Be happy, Regina," he whispered huskily, and then he was gone.

Once the door had closed behind him, he pressed an ear against the heavy oak. He was rewarded by the sound of muffled sobbing.

Captain Lawrence Hunt hurried down the hall to the bedchamber that he shared with his twin brother. Once safely shut inside it, he gave a joyous leap, in the midst of which he kicked his heels together.

Chapter Nine

THE FOLLOWING MORNING DANFORTH ROSE, dressed, and left the bedchamber without disturbing his brother. He had pretended to be asleep while Larry danced his jig the evening before. For, truth to tell, he did not wish to hear how the charade was progressing. He did not really approve of Larry's deception. But he was loath to lecture, for he was certain his twin would not approve of his deception either. It would be a classic case of the pot calling the kettle black.

Obviously Larry was not the only slugabed. Danforth had the breakfast parlor to himself. He was content to make a meal of tea and toast, too troubled to have an appetite. He was on his second cup of the reviving beverage when his peace was shattered by a now familiar crash. This time he hurried toward the hall more from curiosity than alarm.

Anne Welbourne had arrived seconds before him. She was standing, arms akimbo, gazing down at the now battered suit of armor while Master Brougham scrambled for the helmet, which had come to rest beneath a Tudor table.

"Been jousting again, have we, Fitz?" Danforth asked politely. "Sir Lancelot seems to have gotten the worst of it."

"Oh, is that his name?" The little boy's eyes widened.

"Well, it's what my brother and I called him when we were lads."

"I don't think he looks like a Lancelot."

"Certainly not in his present position."

"I would have named him Gawain."

"So be it." Danforth was in the process of restoring the armor to its spot by the stairway. "Now, then, hand me his head." He carefully situated the helmet. "Ah, looks more himself now. If you will give me his sword. Careful. By the hilt, please. It could be sharp."

"Wouldn't cut butter" was the scornful reply.

"Still, it is a good idea on principle." Danforth took the sword from the child's hand and solemnly placed the flat of the blade upon the knight's shoulder. "I dub thee Sir Gawain," he intoned as Anne hid a smile.

"He is supposed to be kneeling" was Fitz's critical observation.

"Don't even consider the possibility. And may I suggest that from now on you think of Sir Gawain as an ally and quit doing battle? He is beginning to look quite battered."

"I never did." The boy was indignant. "We weren't jousting. That was your daft idea. I was decking him."

"I beg your pardon?"

Anne was quicker. She had noticed the sprig of

holly lying on the flagstones. "Oh, of course you were," she exclaimed. "As in 'Deck the halls.' "

Fitz gave her a look of approval. "I was going to put some holly on his helmet. Like a plume, you know. But then he collapsed on me while I was doing it. And after I'd had to go find me own holly, too. Outside. To look at this place, you would never know there was such a thing as Christmas, now, would you? Don't you people ever fa-la-la-la-la?" He glared accusingly.

"Don't look at me. I don't live here. It's all her fault." Danforth grinned wickedly at Anne. "He does have a point, you know. This place does not exactly exude Christmas cheer."

"I know. But Sir Jervis has always considered Christmas greenery just 'sentimental clutter.' And in view of the precarious state of his health, decoration might be unseemly."

"What does he care? Stays in bed all the time, don't he?"

"Score another one for Master Brougham."

"Well," Anne spoke doubtfully, "perhaps he would not object to a bit of holly here and there. After all, we have not had a child here for Christmas in ages."

"That's the spirit. Now, then, why don't you, I, and Fitz here bundle up and go forage?"

"Famous!" The boy beamed. "What are we waiting for?"

The shock of the prodigal's return had almost made Audrey forget about a previous shock. Almost, but not quite. During a wakeful night the vision of her mother's ornate, immensely valuable diamond necklace danced tauntingly before her eyes. She felt she had been dealt a grave injustice. And she was determined to right the wrong as soon as possible. She rose and dressed at an early hour and, forgoing the breakfast parlor, went directly to her father's chamber.

"You again," he growled, returning his teacup to its saucer. "Can't a man be allowed to have his breakfast in peace any longer?"

"It's the price you pay for inviting us to your deathbed." She walked across the room to stand over him.

Not only had Sir Jervis deserted his bed for a chair and a Pembroke table pulled close to the fire, he was fully dressed in a high-collared brown tailcoat, spotted waistcoat, old-fashioned knee breeches, and carpet slippers. He looked remarkably healthy. His daughter said so.

"Looks can deceive." He took a big bite of a Sally Lunn and pointedly failed to ask her to sit down. "The quack who tends me says I could pop off at any minute. And he's determined to help me do so with the physics he prescribes. But I doubt you came to inquire about me health."

"Not solely, anyway." Audrey had decided not to beat about the bush. She took a deep breath and then plunged in. "I came to ask you for a piece of my mother's jewelry."

The old man fixed her with a stare.

"To remember her by," she added lamely.

"Oh. In danger of forgetting your mother, are you? Well, I have a miniature around here somewhere that you can have. 'Twill serve the purpose better than some trinket."

"But you don't understand. Judith has her diamond necklace. It is only fair that I have something as well."

"Judith has the diamonds?" That got the old man's attention. He put down his fork to stare. "But I had thought . . . Just how the devil did that come about?"

"She says that Mama gave it to her on her death-bed."

"Hmmm. Well, there you are then," he said dryly. "Seems you should have been hovering around her, too."

"You know I could not come. I was . . . ill . . . at the time." Her miscarriage was too delicate a matter to speak of.

"Bad luck then." Sir Jervis buttered another roll.

"So now I would like Mama's emeralds."

"Yes, I expect you would. But the fact is, your mother had no emeralds."

"Of course she had. I remember her wearing them many times. They were lovely on her."

"Your mother had no emeralds. Nor any diamonds when it comes to that. She wore the Brougham family jewels."

"Indeed? And what exactly am I if not family?"

"The Dowager Lady Hunt."

"And Judith?"

"What's done is done." He seemed to mull the matter over. "Don't like to snatch the baubles off her neck, as it were. Let her keep 'em for her lifetime. But they are the Brougham family jewels and should remain so. Shouldn't matter all that much to Judith. No need for her to pass 'em down. Elliott, I understand, can deck Regina out with all the jewelry she could ever wear."

"But what is your point? All of your heirs are female—" Audrey stopped abruptly and gave him a searching look. "I see. So that's the way the wind is blowing."

"What the devil does the wind direction have to say to anything?" The old man glared. "But I have had enough of this conversation. I am not about to begin parceling out the family fortune this morning. Plenty of time for that, miss, when I join me ancestors."

"So Chalgrove is no longer disinherited?"

"Mind your own business," he snapped. "Ain't made me mind up about Chalgrove yet. But I do know this, I ain't about to part with any of the family jewels. So if you are short of funds"—he gave her a shrewd look—"I suggest you apply to your lordship stepson. His pockets, so they tell me, are plenty deep." His expression changed suddenly. "Good God!" he ejaculated. "Don't tell me Hunt is up the River Tick!"

"No, of course not." She was at her haughtiest. "Nor am I short of funds. I only want what is rightfully mine. But since you choose to be clutch-fisted, I will bid you good day, sir."

"Well, lah-de-dah," he muttered as he watched her sweep from the room.

After the door had closed, Sir Jervis sat thinking for a moment. Though he would have been loath to admit it, even to himself, he had a soft spot in his heart for his younger daughter. After a bit he walked over to his bed and gave the bell rope a series of short tugs. The summons was answered promptly.

"Johns, go tell Lord Hunt I wish a word with him."

"Lord Hunt is not here at the moment, sir," the butler informed him.

"Not here? Where the devil is there to go? Oh, blast! Hunting again, is he?"

"No, sir. That is to say, not precisely. His lordship and Miss Welbourne have taken Master Fitz on an expedition to collect greenery."

"Greenery, you say? Why the devil would they want to do a fool thing like that?"

"It would seem that Master Fitz desires to deck the halls, sir."

"The devil he does! Well, as soon as they get back tell his lordship I wish to see him.

"Lord Hunt and Anne, eh," he muttered as the servant collected the breakfast things and left. The vision that conjured up served to make his rapidly darkening mood a great deal blacker. It did not brighten after a two-hour wait.

When Lord Hunt at last appeared, his "Good day, sir" was answered with a snapped "Took your own good time, didn't you?"

Danforth's own good mood was not so easily shaken. He had spent a surprisingly pleasant morning in bone-chilling air cutting boughs of holly in the company of a juvenile terror and a soft-spoken young woman with the finest gray eyes he had ever seen. He refused, therefore, to take offense. "I had no idea you wished to see me, sir," he replied mildly.

"Well, I do wish it." Sir Jervis motioned him to a chair beside his own, which was pulled close to the crackling fire. "Want to find out why you're keeping me daughter on such a short rein."

"I beg your pardon?" Danforth moved his chair a bit farther from the blaze before he sat down upon it. "I've no idea what you mean."

"Short of funds. No feather to fly with. Never expected you to turn tight-fisted, lad. Your father was always generous to a fault with Audrey. Of course, if you *are* in the basket, just say so and I'll understand."

"I can assure you," Lord Hunt said stiffly as his good mood slipped, "that my finances are in perfectly good order."

"Just as I thought. Then open your purse, boy."

"I can assure you that Audrey has never lacked—"

"Quit assuring me, dammit," the old man interrupted. "Why else would your stepmama be apply-

71

ing to me for blunt except that you are playing pinchpenny with her?"

Lord Hunt's gorge was beginning to rise, as much from guilt as from Sir Jervis's effrontery. "There is no need for you to concern yourself in this matter, sir," he said icily. "I was not aware that Audrey was applying to you for funds."

"She didn't put it in just that way, of course. Said she wanted her mother's jewelry to remember her by. Balderdash! If that was the case she'd have asked for something when her mother died. Or have waited till I was dead. Which should not be all that long a wait. No, it's plain as a pikestaff that she needs the blunt."

The frost increased in Hunt's tone. "As I was saying, sir, there is no need for you to concern yourself. I will have a word with Audrey."

"See that you do. And soon. I don't like to see me gel made unhappy."

That remark cost Lord Hunt his last vestige of politeness. He rose to his feet and glared down his aristocratic nose. "I can assure you, sir, that your daughter has been far happier with us than she ever was at Stonebridge Park. I bid you good day." He started for the door.

"No need to fly off into the boughs. Stop right there a minute. Got one more thing to say."

His lordship turned reluctantly. "Yes?"

"You should know that it won't do for you to be showing an interest in me ward. For I'll tell you plain. I've other plans for Anne."

Lord Hunt did not bother to reply. But he did shut the door behind him with rather more force than was actually necessary.

Chapter
Ten

THE FAMILY GATHERING AFTER THE EVENING MEAL
was not a festive one in spite of the fact that
the Yule log burned cheerily in the withdrawing-
room fireplace and every portrait, mirror, and
candelabrum was lavishly draped with holly.

At least the guests had had the grace to compliment young Fitz upon the transformation. In response he had launched into a lengthy exposition
on the hardships endured in gathering so much
greenery, a narrative that seemed to require fre-
quent calls upon Lord Hunt to back up his testimony.

Danforth did so absentmindedly. His thoughts
were elsewhere. He was still seething over his interview with Sir Jervis. And though the accusation
of being clutch-fisted with Audrey smarted, being
warned off Anne Welbourne rankled even more.

Not that he was interested in the chit, of course.
She was hardly in his style. It was simply the gall

of the old curmudgeon that incensed him. Nevertheless, his eyes narrowed as he watched Sir Jervis's son stroll over and stand behind Anne, who was seated a bit apart on a sofa reading softly to young Fitz.

"Oh, I say." Chalgrove bent over Anne's shoulder to look at a picture. "That *is* my book. Thought so. Mama used to read it to me when I was your age, Fitz, me lad."

So that was the way the wind was blowing. Danforth felt his irritation grow. He had had his suspicions earlier when Sir Jervis (who had come down for dinner dressed in antique evening clothes but had retired as soon as the meal was over) had seen to it that his son was seated next to his ward. Why, by marrying her to his son, that old devil is going to make certain that Miss Welbourne keeps dancing attendance upon him, he thought. She already seems to be stuck with the bastard.

Meanwhile, Lord Hunt's brother was faring no better in the mood department. All Larry's euphoria from the night before had fled. For he had fully expected that he and Regina would now return to the same happy state of affairs that had existed before he joined the army. Instead the only noticeable result of their brief but passionate lovemaking was that she had stuck close by Elliott all day long and now refused even to glance his way though he had been staring at her for the entire evening.

If Miss Regina Fielding was, or at any rate appeared to be, oblivious of his scrutiny, her mother was not enjoying the same blissful ignorance. In fact, she was becoming increasingly irked by the captain's obsessed interest. Since she could not tell him to redirect his gaze without making a bad matter much worse, she found a different target for her displeasure.

"Chalgrove," she called, thrusting a needle into her tambouring with unnecessary force. "Should not that child be in bed?"

"Can't see why he should be. It's the Christmas season, after all."

"That is no reason to undermine his health. It was bad enough of you to allow him to join the adults for dinner, which I certainly do not approve of. Children should be given a light supper in their nursery and then put to bed."

"Oh, having Fitz join us for dinner was Papa's idea, not mine. Expect he wanted the chance to become acquainted with his only grandson."

"Humph!" Whether Mrs. Fielding was responding to the implied criticism of her failure to produce a male offspring or to the dubious status of her father's grandson, the listeners could only guess.

"Be that as it may"—she jabbed fiercely at her embroidery once more—"there is no reason for him to still be up."

Surprisingly, the object of the discussion seemed to think she had a point. "Don't you people here ever *do* anything?" he inquired plaintively.

"We are a dull lot, that's true." Audrey, who had been strumming softly on the pianoforte, smiled at the lad. "Were we always this dull, Chalgrove?"

"Not a bit of it," her brother replied. "We used to get up to all sorts of larks. Just look outside now, will you?" He strolled over to the window, where frost was sparkling on the panes. "I thought so. There's a full moon. And it's cold enough to freeze the tail off a brass monkey. What does that make you think of, big sister?"

Audrey clapped her hands together. "The pond! I had not thought of it in years. But the pond must be frozen."

They had everyone's attention.

"What are you two on about?" Regina asked. "I know the pond, of course. And that ponds do freeze. But why the excitement?"

"Skating, little niece, skating!" Chalgrove exclaimed.

"Oh, yes." Audrey turned toward her sister. "Remember, Judith? It was practically a Christmas tradition. When we came home from boarding school for the holidays there would always be one evening—Christmas itself once or twice as I recall—when we would take our skates and build a bonfire—"

"Yes, and roast chestnuts and apples over it," Chalgrove interrupted.

"And we'd come home to mulled cider," Audrey finished. "I had almost forgot that . . ." What she did not go on to say aloud was that she had forgotten there had ever been good times at Stonebridge Park.

"Well, what are we waiting for?" Fitz was on his feet.

"Do not be absurd." His aunt Judith frowned. "It is entirely too late for such an outing."

"Why?"

"I wonder if the pond actually is frozen." Anne spoke quickly to ward off the scold forming on Mrs. Fielding's lips. "This is the first truly cold day we have had."

"Well, we can soon settle that." Chalgrove started toward the bellpull. But before he reached it, the butler, bearing a tea board, appeared as if by magic. "Oh, I say, Johns," Chalgrove exclaimed, "is the pond frozen yet?"

"Why, I believe so, sir." Johns carefully set his tray upon a table near the fire. "I believe one of the footmen did mention it."

"Hard enough to skate on?"

"I really could not say, sir, but I will inquire of Peter. I should think, though, that it would require another day of this hard freeze to be entirely safe."

"Well, then," Chalgrove declared as he helped himself to fruitcake, "it is settled. We will go skating tomorrow night. Come and pour out, Judith."

"Are there any skates still around, Johns?" Audrey asked the retreating butler as they all moved toward the tea board.

"I am sure we can find a sufficient number." His eyes swept the group.

"To fit me?" Fitz asked anxiously.

"Oh, yes. I am quite certain that the skates your father used as a lad are in the attic."

"Famous! Of course," the boy added doubtfully, "I have never skated. It can't be too hard, though, can it? I mean to say, so many people do it." The words were directed toward Miss Welbourne.

"Not a bit of it," she assured him. "I will teach you."

Danforth, who had moved to stand beside her, did not look pleased by her kind offer. While he was rather taken with young Fitz himself, he did not wish to see Anne developing maternal feelings in that direction.

"Oh, I say, Captain," Chalgrove said when they had all settled down to the business of refreshment, "this is a bit hard on you, I collect." He tried without much effect to look guilty. "Our planning a skating party, I mean to say, when you can't participate." He gestured with his cup at the soldier's leg, stretched out stiffly in front of him.

"Not a bit of it." Larry, who had been thinking much the same thing, smiled gallantly. "I shall enjoy watching.

"Besides, I shall not be the only nonparticipant. You won't be skating either, will you, sir?"

The words were directed at Lord Elliott, who choked on the cake he was eating.

"Of course he will be." Audrey gave her stepson a repressive look. "I recall from my winter visit with Arabella that you are a marvelous skater, Edwin."

"I think your son was implying that I am now too decrepit for such exercise," his lordship replied dryly.

"Oh, nothing of the kind, sir," the captain protested a bit too heartily. "I just thought such frolics might have little appeal at . . ." His voice trailed off.

"At my age? Well, actually, I am quite looking forward to the outing. A case of second childhood one must suppose."

Regina was glaring daggers at her former sweetheart. But it was her mother who brought the subject to a close. "Well, I, for one, have no intention of bringing on a severe case of the grippe—or worse—by exposing myself to this frost. And you should all be well advised to have second thoughts about such an outing."

"Old spoilsport," Fitz said underneath his breath.

Later, while the tea things were being cleared, Audrey managed to draw her younger stepson aside. "I wish a word with you, Lawrence."

"Now?"

"Yes, now. You have managed to elude me on every other occasion. I will take no further chances." She led him to the settee on the far side of the room, out of earshot. "Now explain yourself, sir," she said softly but with a hint of steel in her voice. There was a fixed smile on her face for the benefit of anyone who might be watching.

"I don't know what you mean."

Her brows rose. "You walk in here—no, I beg your pardon, you *limp* in here with a brand-new cane and a patch over your eye and you don't know what I mean when I ask for an explanation? Well, never mind all that." She sighed. "For it is quite obvious what you are trying to do, and I want you to stop it."

"Why should I? All's fair in love, et cetera. And he is wrong for her."

"He is nothing of the sort. Lord Elliott is a wonderful man and will make Regina a wonderful husband."

"What you mean is, he is a wonderful catch. I never expected you would think like your sister, Audrey."

"I am not thinking like Judith." Her tone made a travesty of her smile. "I just happen to believe that the two of them are quite well suited, and I do not like to see you upsetting my niece this way. They are betrothed, Larry." She now spoke gently. "The notice has been published. What's done is done. I realize this is hard for you. But you must make the best of it. There will be other loves. Trust me."

"Should I?" He looked at her curiously. "It has never occurred to me to wonder before, but were you happy with my father?"

Her chin went up. "I most certainly was."

"Well, you always seemed to be," he admitted. "You certainly made our lives happy. Which brings me to something *I* wish to inquire of *you*. That is, if you have quite finished ringing a peal over me," he added politely.

"I will cease if you will promise to think over what I have said."

"I promise."

"And go back to London?"

"Don't push it too far, Audrey. Let's talk about you now. Why are you so unhappy?"

"Unhappy? Do you have maggots in your head? I am nothing of the sort."

"Perhaps I have chosen the wrong word then. Preoccupied? Bothered? But something is troubling you. You have changed. I noticed it the moment I came home."

"Of course I have changed." She grimaced. "I am growing older. After all, you must realize that I am a contemporary of poor, dear, decrepit Lord Elliott."

"Touché. And so, I take it, you are not going to confide in me."

"There is nothing to confide, my dear, dear Larry." Her smile was tremulous. "Now, shall we go to bed? Everyone else has, as you may have noticed."

Chapter Eleven

WHEN THE SKATING PARTY ARRIVED AT THE POND the following evening, Captain Hunt was already there waiting. He had ridden over earlier with a groom who had first built a fire, then led the captain's horse back to the stables. He was now leaning heavily on his cane while dejectedly tossing sticks into the roaring bonfire. There was a brave smile upon his face as he welcomed the others, but his single eye looked sad.

The night could not have been more perfect. The moon shed a clear white light over the scene, sparkling upon the oval sheet of ice and illuminating the diamond-encrusted evergreens behind it. "Tom examined the pond before he left," Larry told the skaters. "He says it might be a touch iffish in the very center, but the outer part should hold up a brigade. Good skating." His smile grew braver still.

"Oh, this really is famous!" So stating, Fitz ran around the bonfire for several laps whooping all the way, then sat down and began struggling with his skates. In the latter instance the rest of the party, sans the captain, followed his example.

Lord Elliott was first on the ice. While the others watched, he skirted the perimeter of the pond at remarkable speed. "The ice is perfect," he called as he whizzed by the watchers. "Smooth as glass." And to demonstrate he began to cut a series of circles and figure eights, first on one foot and then on the other, backward for a while, then forward.

"He really is quite good, is he not? For an antiquarian." Audrey smiled at her stepson.

"He would be," the captain growled beneath his breath.

"I'm ready!" Fitz shouted as he stood up, teetering dangerously.

"Hold it a minute, sport." Danforth gave a final tug to his own skate strap, then went to the child's assistance. "I think we need a bit of adjustment here. Sit back down a minute."

"You've got the points in the back, boy." Fitz's father laughed as he took, rather shakily, to the ice. "Won't do. Unless you plan to skate in that direction all night long."

Anne had come to Danforth's aid and was untangling the straps of the child's left foot while he coped with the right. She was looking uncommonly pretty, he thought, with the sharp air turning her cheeks—and nose—pink and her eyes sparkling with pleasure. It occurred to him that there must be very little fun in Anne Welbourne's life.

"All set?" She nodded and together they hoisted Fitz to his feet, which immediately flew out from underneath him. "Steady on, lad," Danforth said, laughing, as he tightened his grip. The child righted himself for one brief moment, then was once again prevented from landing on his backside.

"It's s-slippery!"

"That is the whole idea. Come on now. We won't let you fall."

Between them Danforth and Anne guided the child out upon the ice, where he gradually began to steady. "I'm skating," he crowed. "I say, this is famous."

"It really is," Anne agreed, smiling across his head at Danforth. That expert skater became suddenly quite unsteady on his feet.

Regina had gone to sit on a log by the pond's edge to put on her skates. But in spite of the pretty spectacle the others made in the moonlight she found that she had little heart for the exercise. "Do hurry, Regina," Audrey called as she skated past. "I had forgotten how much fun this is."

"Just a minute."

Regina had made the mistake of glancing back over her shoulder once again at the solitary spectator by the bonfire. "I'm freezing. I'll just warm myself before I start."

She made a great show of removing her gloves and holding her hands to the flames as she stood beside the captain. Her voice trembled a bit as she spoke. "I am so sorry that you cannot skate with the rest of us."

"Oh, I don't mind very much." His eye was on the sparks as they streamed skyward. "Do you know what I have been thinking of?"

"What?"

"That time I taught you to skate. Do you remember?"

"Oh, yes," she breathed. "That is, I had quite forgot till you mentioned it."

"Had you, indeed?" he said softly, this time gazing directly into her face. She returned the gaze but could not help flinching at the sight of the black eyepatch. "You are very fortunate then, Gina. I cannot forget a moment of our time together. The apple orchard especially. Don't tell me you have forgot the apple blossoms, Regina. I don't think I could bear that. Along with everything else."

"Don't, please." Tears were gathering in her eyes.

"You can't marry him, Gina." The words came rushing out, seemingly against his will. "You can't. You don't love him. You cannot possibly love him."

"Please. You mustn't. I—"

"Regina!"

Whatever she might have said was cut short by her aunt's preemptive call. "Hurry up. We need you. We are going to form a chain."

"Coming!"

With a last sorrowful look at the maimed hero, Regina hurried toward the ice.

Chalgrove placed himself at the head of the chain and his sister took his hand. "What are we waiting for?"

"Come on"—Danforth steered Fitz by the shoulders—"we'll hold you. You won't fall."

"You first," he said to Anne, and she grasped Audrey's hand, putting the child between them. Regina came next, with Elliott taking the whip-end spot.

Chalgrove started off quite sedately, but he soon accelerated. The chain sped around the pond at a merry clip, the links laughing and shouting to one another as it went.

"Damn it all, anyhow," Larry muttered as he watched. He flung another stick into the flames with a force that sent the sparks spiraling to the heavens, reminiscent of the fireworks that had celebrated Waterloo. He was beginning to regret the charade that was keeping him away from all the fun. Especially since it showed no sign of accomplishing its purpose. He cursed again as he watched Regina laugh back over her shoulder at something Elliott must have said.

The skating grew wilder and wilder. No longer content merely with speed, Chalgrove began to zigzag, maneuvering his chain like a coachman's whip. The skaters were snaked this way and that with Elliott taking the full brunt of the whip's crack and Regina only slightly less involved. There was much laughter and shouting from everyone, but Fitz's treble ranged above it all as he squealed in a mixture of fear and joy while his skates for much of the time simply stroked the air as Anne and Danforth supported him between them.

"Oh, do stop, Chalgrove," Audrey pleaded with her failing breath. "I'm d-dying."

Brotherlike, he continued the whip-cracking for another turn around the pond before finally coming to a stop.

"That was famous, Papa!" Without thinking, Fitz attempted to jump up and down. Since Anne and Danforth no longer held him, he found himself suddenly scooting on his bottom across the ice. "Let's do it again!" he whooped as he slid past his sire.

"Not for a fortune," Audrey gasped. "I cannot tell you how grateful I feel not to have broken every last bone in my body."

"Fustian. You loved it and you know it," her brother retorted. "No one would suspect that you are practically a crone."

"Thank you very much for that left-handed compliment. Age has not improved your tact, I see."

"My, aren't we prickly. Come on, brat." Chalgrove hoisted his son to his wobbly feet. "Let an expert teach you. Here, Anne, you take his other hand."

"Will you come skate with me? Sedately?" Lord

Elliott smiled down at his fiancée, who had been struggling to regain her breath.

"With pleasure," she replied. "That is, if 'sedately' is a solemn vow."

"On my word as a gentleman." He placed a hand over his heart, then offered it to Regina. They skated off gracefully and slowly, together, following Anne and Chalgrove, with Fitz now wobbling on his own power between them.

"Well, that only leaves you and me, my son," Audrey observed as she skated up to Danforth.

He did not appear to hear her. His narrowed eyes were focused on Anne and Chalgrove, who had now crossed hands and were engaged in cutting complicated figures in the ice.

"Danforth, wake up!"

"Oh? I beg your pardon?"

"I have just remarked that there are only the two of us left. Ergo, come skate with your stepmama, Lord Hunt."

"Very well."

"That was certainly gracious," she said, laughing, as she took his proffered hand and they joined the procession. "What has put you into such a taking? You look almost as dog-in-the-mangerish as your brother."

"Me? In a taking? Don't be doltish."

"And don't you bite my head off, young man. You may be—Oh, my heavens!" She was following his glare to its target. Mr. Brougham and Miss Welbourne were now engaged in cutting a figure eight while Fitz, left on his own, was attempting to skate backward despite the fact that his forward motion was still disaster-prone. "Is the wind blowing that way, then? Don't tell me that you have formed a *tendre* for my young cousin."

"Don't be absurd."

"Am I being? Then why else is your nose so out of joint?"

"It isn't. Or if it is, I expect it's because I resent the fact that your old horror of a father is throwing Miss Welbourne at your brother's head. She is far too good for that here-and-thereian."

Audrey came to a full stop, causing her partner to stumble.

"Papa is doing that?" she asked when he'd regained his equilibrium. "I'll not believe it. Whatever gave you such a notion?"

"He did. He warned me off, in fact. Seemed to think I was interested in her myself. Though what put that particular maggot in his head, God only knows."

"Chalgrove and Anne," Audrey mused, more to herself than to her stepson. "What can Papa be thinking of? Or is it Papa's doing? She is, after all, the one who wrote the invitations to all of us. Well, well. Still waters do run deep, they say."

"If you are implying that Anne has set her cap for your rackety brother, I, for one, refuse to believe it."

She looked up, amazed at his vehemence. "You really are smitten, aren't you?"

"Of course not. I just happen to admire the young lady, that's all."

I think I am beginning to admire her, too. Audrey did not share the thought aloud. But her sister's suspicion that quiet, demure little Miss Welbourne was indeed scheming for Sir Jervis's fortune began to fester in her mind. She and Danforth glided on in silence, both occupied with their own private thoughts.

The skating party soon broke up and headed for the bonfire. Larry backed away a bit, relinquishing his place to the frozen skaters. Only Lord Elliott, the first to take the ice, remained upon it, perhaps to prove a point. Larry watched the older man glumly while his lordship practiced a series of intricate maneuvers. He was the sole audience for the skillful performance. All of the others, Regina included, had their attention riveted on the flames as they sought to bring life back into freezing toes and fingers. He was, therefore, the only one to become concerned when Elliott's graceful, one-footed glides carried him closer and closer to the center of the pond. He was just about to call out a warning when he heard an ominous crack and saw Elliott disappear quicker than thought beneath the shattered ice.

"He's gone under!" he shouted, sprinting toward the pond and flinging off his greatcoat as he ran, then sliding swiftly across the ice on his leather boot soles. He approached the gaping hole more warily, however, prone and sliding on his stomach, acutely aware of an ominous cracking as he drew near the opening close enough to peer down into the frigid black water. There was no sign of Lord Elliott. Larry eased himself carefully into the hole, trying to do no further damage to the ring of ice.

Danforth and Chalgrove had been close behind him. They now slid in tandem on their stomachs. "Hold my ankles and let's get closer," Danforth commanded hoarsely, and the two men inched forward on the ice. The moments after Larry disappeared into the pond seemed interminable, and Danforth had just decided to go in after him when two heads bobbed up, gasping, through the icy hole. The captain was clutching Lord Elliott by the collar.

Getting the two men out of the water proved difficult. The rescue was hampered by heavy, waterlogged clothing and an icy ledge that tended to break off in chunks underneath their weight. But to the immense relief of the horrified watchers on the bank, the rescue was, at last, accomplished.

"Quick, get them to the fire before they freeze," Danforth barked, and he and Chalgrove hustled the two men across the frozen pond, their wet clothes stiffening as they went. The rescuers thrust the victims close to the blaze while the ladies draped them with the group's accumulated coats and shawls.

"Th-th-thank you," Lord Elliott said to Captain Hunt as soon as his teeth stopped chattering sufficiently to speak. "I don't think I could have lasted very much longer. I was totally disoriented. Couldn't find the blasted hole. Lucky for me you acted so quickly. I—" He stopped suddenly, a mystified look on his face. "I say, Captain. Haven't you had a rather miraculous recovery?"

Everyone had been gazing at Larry with reverential looks upon their faces appropriate for viewing a hero who had just pulled a fellow human being from the jaws of death. Now these expressions were undergoing a marked change.

None more so than Regina Fielding's. She had made the transition from hero worship to black suspicion in record time. She now walked around her fiancé's shivering form to stand next to the dripping captain, to reach up and jerk off the sodden satin patch. She found herself staring into *two* blue, healthy but wary eyes.

"You . . . you . . . humbug!"

The slap Miss Fielding administered to the captain's cheek cracked sharply, like breaking ice, in the still and frosty air.

Chapter Twelve

"K ER-CHOO!"

A sneeze reverberated throughout the room.

"God bless you." The voice came from the doorway.

Lawrence Hunt had risen early after a restless night. He had sought the solitude of the library and the solace of the *Gazette* to still his racing thoughts. Lord Elliott was not a welcome sight.

As he entered the room and joined the younger man by the fire, Elliott applied a handkerchief to his nose. "May I?" Without waiting for permission he sat down in the wing chair opposite the one Lawrence occupied. "I cannot tell you how relieved I am to hear you sneeze." He returned the handkerchief to his pocket. "It would really be the final ignominy to be the only one to get the grippe from our icy bath."

"That's nonsense." Lawrence made no attempt to hide his irritation.

"Oh, no, it isn't. Not a bit of it. For you must admit you have been at considerable pains to make me appear decrepit. Having you be the one to pull me from a watery grave is, I readily admit, hard to accept. I mean to speak to your brother and Chalgrove about their laggard behavior." His smile was a bit forced.

"Do that. If one of them had decided to play the hero, it would have saved a great deal of awkwardness all around."

"Exactly. That is why I have sought you out this morning to thank you properly for your sacrifice in dragging me out of the pond."

Lawrence waved away the gratitude. "Your thanks are not needed. Believe me, my action was a reflex. Besides, you would have gotten yourself out if I had not plugged up the hole with my own stupid body."

"I rather doubt it." For a moment Elliott looked ill. "And thanks *are* needed, for you paid a heavy price for your . . . gallantry. You must be cursing—"

"Oh, there you are!" A piping voice cut short the conversation as Master Brougham entered the library like a small whirlwind. He planted himself in front of Captain Hunt and stared at him fixedly. "I wished particularly to see you," he announced after several seconds of scrutiny.

"Well, you are certainly doing just that," Lawrence retorted. "Did no one ever tell you it is not polite to stare?"

"Where's your eye patch?"

"In my bedchamber."

"Can I have it?"

"Yes, you little ghoul."

Fitz's gaze refused to waver.

"It is on my dressing table, to be exact. Now run and get it. You are making me most uncomfortable."

"Did your eye get well then?"

"Indeed. Miraculously."

"That's a whisker, ain't it?"

"Yes. An outright lie, in fact."

"If you didn't need to wear a patch, why did you?"

"As a matter of fact," Lord Elliott broke in, "the captain and I were just about to explore that subject when you interrupted us."

"So why did you wear it?"

"That is none of your business, brat. Now go."

"I'll bet a monkey you didn't need the cane either. You didn't limp a bit when you ran across the ice."

"Aren't you the observant one. Scoot!"

"Papa says you were just pretending to be wounded. Papa says you most likely weren't even at Waterloo. Papa says—"

"Go!"

There was the same ring of authority in the captain's voice that had sent men charging into battle. Even Fitz was impressed enough to head reluctantly for the door. He hesitated, though, upon the threshold. "Since you don't have any more use for it, can I have the cane as well?"

"No, you cannot!" the captain thundered. Fitz scurried out the door.

"Enterprising little scrub, isn't he?" Elliott observed.

"Well, I collect I have it coming." Lawrence's sigh came up from the soles of his Hessian boots. "That and whatever it is you are about to say."

"Young Fitz covered a lot of my territory. As he pointed out, the heart of the matter is 'Why?'"

"You need to ask?" Lawrence's voice was bitter.

"No, not really. It was obvious that you were

bringing up the heavy artillery. Being close to Regina in age and a former sweetheart made you a dangerous rival. But a wounded hero as well ... I don't mind admitting that you cost me anxious moments."

"Till my artillery blew up in my face? Well, it was a daft idea in the first place. Wounded war heroes are no match for belted earls."

"Viscount, actually."

"Whatever. The principle remains the same."

"Then why don't we leave it like that?" Elliott said softly. "You had your chance, Captain Hunt, or so I have been told. Now Regina is betrothed to me. I plan to make her happy. Let's call a truce then, shall we?"

"Are you warning me off?"

"Nothing quite so dramatic. I am simply asking you to accept the situation."

"Just lick my imaginary wounds and crawl off, eh?"

"Here again your flair for hyperbole oversets my prosaic message. But color it any way you wish. I am asking you to leave Regina alone. A request, by the by, that may be superfluous. She is not, I collect, exactly in charity with you at the moment."

The captain winced as he recalled the slap. "True. But I must warn you, Lord Elliott, that young Fitz was dead wrong on one count. I actually was at Waterloo. Which means I am not good at recognizing lost causes. I do not, sir, give up easily."

"I see." Elliott rose to his feet. "Then may the best man win."

"No, by damn." The other met his eyes. "Let whoever win who can."

* * *

Once again Miss Welbourne and Lord Hunt were the only residents of the park who responded to the crash. The sound was now a familiar one, evoking little interest. The servants, busy with their morning tasks, would deal with the matter when the proper time came to tidy up the hall. Anne feared that young Fitz might have hurt himself. Danforth just happened to be coming down the stairs.

"What are you up to now, you little horror?" He watched the helmet bang its way across the tiles. "Can't you leave that armor alone? Doesn't seem right for it to have survived the Saracens or whoever and now be done in by a halfling who won't do what he is told." He turned at the sound of footsteps behind him. "Oh, good morning, Miss Welbourne. No need for alarm. It's only Master Brougham up to his old tricks again."

"I am no such thing." Fitz had retrieved the helmet and turned to face them. Anne gasped, then smothered a giggle. "I just bumped into him, that's all. Accidental-like."

"Take that damned thing off!" Danforth roared. "And put it right back where you pinched it."

"He said I could have it." Fitz's chin stuck out. "You just go and ask him. He don't need it one bit. His eye ain't gone at all." There was no mistaking the disappointment in his voice. "Thought there'd be nothing but a hole in his head, but no. He's got two perfectly good orbs. Can see every bit as good as you can."

"And a whole lot better than you, young man." Anne brushed past Danforth on the stairs to see to Fitz. He had tied the patch's ribbon straight across his face. It was forcing down the lid of the "uninjured" eye. "What did you do, blunder into Sir Whoever there because you couldn't see him?"

94

He nodded. "Well, I saw him a little," he amended, "but he was much closer than I thought."

"I see. And did Captain Hunt really say you could have the eye patch?"

"Course he did. It ain't no use to him now, is it?"

"Then may he keep it?" She looked up at Danforth.

"Oh, why not," he said, capitulating. "Only I'd stay away from your cousin Regina if I were you. It could be a bit like waving a red cape in front of an angry bull."

"Oh, really? Did she ask for it? Well, she can't have it. Captain Hunt gave it to me. For keeps." Fitz squirmed while Anne made the proper adjustments to the eye patch, then scampered toward the stairs. He was halfway up when a thought struck and he came to a sudden halt. "Hey, you, down there."

"Are you addressing me?" His lordship's voice was frosty.

"Are you really the captain's twin brother?"

"Yes."

"Are you sure? Twins are supposed to look just alike and you don't look any more like Captain Hunt than I do."

"I am sure."

"For one thing, he is a whole lot taller."

"Is there a point to this conversation?"

Anne hid a smile at his lordship's starchy tone.

"I was thinking that if you really are his twin you might ask him to give me his cane as well. He don't need a cane any more than he needs an eye patch. There ain't nothing in the world wrong with—"

"Go!" Lord Hunt interrupted with a murderous look.

"Well, he *don't* need it," Fitz muttered as he raced up the stairs.

"Oh, my." Anne shook her head in despair. "He really is full of energy, isn't he?"

"He's full of something." His lordship glared.

"Oh, come now. You mustn't be too hard on him. It's difficult to be a child in an invalid's household surrounded by a pack of grown-ups."

"Getting fond of him, are we?" Danforth scowled as he once more helped her replace the armor.

"Fond of Fitz?" She looked thoughtful. "I hadn't considered it, but, yes, he is rather endearing."

"Indeed? I had not noticed."

Anne gave him a curious look and elected to change the subject. "How is Captain Hunt this morning?" she inquired politely.

"You need to ask? He is, as you saw—and young Fitz observed—completely recovered. He sees. He walks. He's a veritable miracle."

"I meant," she said patiently, still wondering what had put him in so foul a mood, "how is he after his icy bath?"

"Sneezing a bit, that's all. Really none the worse for wear. At least not from his ducking. Otherwise . . ." He shrugged.

"I see. 'Otherwise.' If it is not too presumptuous a question," she asked as they walked together toward the breakfast room, "just what is the relationship between the captain and Regina?"

He was slow in answering.

She colored a bit. "Forgive me. I had no right to ask."

"No, no. Of course you have the right. You need to know what is going on under your roof. The thing is, I am not too sure myself. I suppose you could say they were once sweethearts. But I never thought it was anything but a mooncalf affair. They

96

were barely out of leading strings. And he was eager enough, when the time came, to join the army. So?" He shrugged again. "Deuced if I know how to answer you."

"A mooncalf romance," she mused. "It's said that a first love is hardest to get over."

He glanced down curiously. "You speak from experience, do you?"

"Oh, no. Only from what I have heard—and read. But you are a man of the world. Perhaps you can say."

Danforth was relieved that the presence of his stepmother and her sister in the breakfast parlor made it impossible for him to answer. For some reason, which he left unexplored, he did not wish Anne to know just how little "a man of the world" he actually was.

Chapter Thirteen

LORD ELLIOTT HAD PICKED UP LAWRENCE'S ABAN-
doned *Gazette* and settled back down in front of
the fireplace to read it. But his eyes were on the
crackling flames and not the printed page when
Audrey came into the library and saw him there.

"All alone, Edwin?" she asked unnecessarily as
she returned a copy of *Emma* to the shelves.
"Where is Regina?" She walked over to join him.

"In her bedchamber. Feeling unwell. Again.
Strange, isn't it, how your stepson's miraculous recovery has brought about a relapse in your niece?"

"Oh, dear. I am indeed sorry." She sat down on
the edge of the chair that Lawrence had vacated,
distressed by Lord Elliott's tone. "I could murder
the boy for such a tasteless prank. It was all in fun,
I've little doubt. Larry was always a jokester. But
this time he should have realized that he was causing real distress."

"A *prank*, Audrey? Funning? Oh, I think not.

There was method in his mischief." He paused for a denial that did not come. "Tell me, did you know what he was up to?"

"No, of course not. Or I would have stopped him."

"Then it is a pity he did not confide in you," he said dryly.

"Oh, I know what you are thinking. I should have unmasked him the moment he limped in. Unpatched him, that is." To her horror, she actually giggled. "But to tell you the truth, I was struck speechless at first. And then it seemed too late. But in your case it has all turned out for the best, has it not? For if Larry wished to work on Regina's sympathy, the scheme backfired. She now despises him."

"Does she, indeed? Or is it a case of 'the lady doth protest too much'?"

"Oh, come now, Edwin. You are taking this far too seriously."

"Perhaps you are right." He sighed. "The truth is, it is very lowering to be rescued by one's rival."

Her voice was a bit unsteady as she replied, "Be that as it may, the alternative is unthinkable."

"Thank you. And I realize I am being very mean-spirited to wish it had been someone else who came haring to the rescue. Why could one of the others not have fished me out?"

"Well, presumedly because they were all busy taking off their skates. Larry just happened to be the only one unoccupied and watching."

"I know. And that, my dear Audrey, is why I find this whole business so lowering. I was trying to prove my youth, you see, by skating better—and longer—than anyone else. Pride certainly went before a fall in my case."

"Oh, for heaven's sake, Edwin," she scolded, "I do wish you would not go on and on about your age. You make yourself out to be Methuselah. It certainly dampens my spirits since we are contemporaries."

"It should not." His appraisal of her was admiring. "For no one would believe we are close in age. You look . . . marvelous, Audrey. As beautiful—no, more so—than when I first saw you."

"Don't give me your Spanish coin, Edwin," she said, laughing. "No, I take that back. It is a dead giveaway to my advanced age that I lap up flummery like a cat with cream."

"It isn't flummery but God's own truth. Tell me something, Audrey," he asked seriously. "You have been widowed for ages. How does it happen that you have never married again? It certainly cannot be from any lack of suitors."

"I really can't say," she mused. "I have had some gentlemen friends who, with a bit of encouragement, would have gone down on one knee. Well"— she smiled—"two actually did without any encouragement. But there was never anyone for whom I would have traded the life I had. The twins and I rubbed along very well together, you see. I like to think that I was needed. If you asked them, however, they would say that they were the ones who took care of me."

"To the extent of scaring away would-be suitors?"

"Not a bit of it!" she said hotly, then laughed. "Oh, well, then, there was one particular fop that Larry discouraged by spilling ratafia on the lavender coat that was his pride and joy."

"I see. Another of his delightful pranks?"

"No! Oh, very well then, yes. He was a mere child and I was grateful. It saved me the awkwardness of having to dampen the gentleman's ardor. And it was an isolated incident. The twins always wished the best for me. You are determined, are you not, to cast them—or Larry, at any rate—in the worst possible light?"

"Perhaps," he admitted. "I can also understand how, growing up, they might have been loath to share you. However, they will soon be setting up their own households, I should think. What then, Audrey?"

"I don't know." Her face was suddenly bleak.

"Perhaps you should try to be a bit more receptive to the next suitor who comes along."

"Perhaps I should. Only you see, Edwin, it is most unlikely there will be another suitor."

"Fustian." His voice was scornful.

The entrance of a housemaid armed with a feather duster and broom brought an end to the conversation. Perhaps fortunately. Otherwise Audrey feared that she might have found herself confessing all her folly to this sympathetic friend. And she really would have hated, she afterward reflected, to lower herself in his admiring eyes.

As the day wore on, Captain Lawrence Hunt concluded that he might as well be wearing a bell around his neck and forced to cry out "Unclean! Unclean!" when anyone came into view. Certainly he was being treated like a leper. Mrs. Fielding pretended not to see him when they passed; even so, her sniff was eloquent. His stepmama merely shook her head sorrowfully when their paths crossed. "I shall endeavor not to say I told you so," she said.

"That's good, for actually you didn't."

"Only because you did not afford me the opportunity. Had I known what you were up to, I should certainly have warned you off. And as it was, I surely managed to convey my disapproval of your charade."

"Oh, indeed. You certainly did do that."

"I am glad you can admit it." She had hurried on to her bedchamber, her point well made.

Chalgrove Brougham chuckled and winked knowingly whenever they happened to meet. And the sight of young Fitz wearing his eye patch and limping heavily (on a stick that one of the gardeners had provided) was enough to make the Waterloo veteran snarl and gnash his teeth. But it was Miss Regina Fielding who applied the *coup de grâce*. He had knocked softly upon her chamber door, ready with a much-rehearsed apology for his shabby conduct.

"You!" she exclaimed furiously as she slammed the door shut to the peril of his nose.

So at the conclusion of a seemingly interminable day, it was much in the manner of a man about to go into a battle where the odds were stacked heavily against him that he put the final touches to his cravat and descended the stairs to join the other Christmas guests of Stonebridge Park.

The atmosphere had not noticeably improved. As he entered the withdrawing room Regina pointedly turned her back to talk automatically and unintelligibly to her fiancé.

"Well, if it ain't our invalid." Chalgrove slapped his knee with laughter. "Glad to see you so wonderfully recovered."

It was Anne who tactfully pulled the attention away from the cavalry veteran by giving a progress report on Sir Jervis's health. His doctor had paid another visit and was very encouraging. He'd concluded that the stimulation of company was what the old gentleman had needed all along. Of course, she said with a smile, Sir Jervis had informed Dr. Ward that he was an addlepated quack who had not the slightest notion of what he was about. The doctor had stuck to his guns, however, and suggested that Sir Jervis join them for dinner again. It was doubtful that he would do so, but perhaps . . . "Oh, maybe this is he." She turned at the sound of the door opening.

It was not Sir Jervis, however, but his eldest daughter who appeared, white-faced and agitated. Mrs. Fielding stood in the doorway, her mouth working but unable to utter a sound.

"Mama, what is it?" Regina hurried to her side.

"It is gone!" she managed to croak.

"Gone?" Regina looked bewildered.

"Stolen!"

The voice was gaining power.

"What are you talking about, Mama? Compose yourself and tell us."

"My necklace!"

Wild eyes looked from one to another of the stunned occupants of the withdrawing room. "The diamond necklace that my mother gave me on her deathbed. It has disappeared." She drew in a deep breath. "Someone in this house has stolen it."

Chapter Fourteen

THERE WAS A SHOCKED SILENCE. ANNE WAS THE FIRST to break it. "Oh, surely you must simply have mislaid it, Mrs. Fielding. After dinner I will help you look."

"Do not patronize me, young lady. Do you think I have not looked in every possible place? I tell you, someone has taken it." She glared. "I want the servants searched. Immediately."

"Our servants have been with us forever, Mrs. Fielding." Anne spoke calmly, refusing to be intimidated. "And in some cases their parents and grandparents were employed here before them, as you should know. Their honesty is not to be questioned."

"You take far too much upon yourself, Miss Welbourne. As a daughter of this house, I think my authority exceeds yours."

"And I think this is a matter for Sir Jervis to decide. Though I dislike to have him bothered with it, for I am certain that he will not countenance having his servants insulted."

"She is right, Mama," Regina interposed soothingly. "You must not fling accusations around. Your necklace is bound to show up."

"Bound to show up? Bound to show up? What do you expect it to do, Regina, sprout limbs and walk?"

Fitz, who had been watching, bug-eyed, unfortunately laughed.

Mrs. Fielding wheeled toward the hearth, where he was seated. Her look of fury at such inappropriate levity underwent a startling metamorphosis. It became the dawning of understanding. "You!" she exclaimed.

"M-me?" Fitz sobered instantly.

"Yes, you. You were in my bedchamber. Admit it."

"Oh, for goodness' sake, Judith," Audrey intervened, "the child has been in everybody's chamber. He is merely curious."

"Just one minute!" Chalgrove Brougham bristled as he glared at his oldest sister. An indifferent parent at most times, he was not about to allow his son to be called a thief. He now said so in no uncertain terms.

"If you are implying that the lad here stole your demmed necklace, well, then, you had best apologize. Fitz may have his faults, but, by God, thievery ain't one of them."

"Oh, I am sure Mother did not mean to imply . . ." Regina's face was distressed as she looked from one irate sibling to the other.

"Demmed if she didn't. She accused the boy in front of the whole company." He stared around at the embarrassed faces for confirmation. "She always was a holier-than-thou prig, thinking the worst of everybody, and I can see that age ain't changed a thing."

"Oh, do come down from your high horse, Chalgrove. I did not accuse the boy of theft."

"Then what would you call it?"

"I merely suspect that while he was prowling in my bedchamber—and I take it that only a 'holier-than-thou prig' would object to that," she interposed with heavy sarcasm, "he saw the necklace and pocketed it as he would any geegaw that caught his fancy—a marble, a robin's egg, a piece of string. I do not believe for a minute that he knew the value of it. I will even go so far as to say that it did not seem wrong to him to help himself to a pretty thing."

"I do, too, know the difference 'twix a necklace and a robin's egg," Fitz countered belligerently.

"What I am saying, Fitzgerald"—with an effort Mrs. Fielding reined in her temper and attempted to cajole—"is that if you will simply return the necklace, we will say no more about it."

"I ain't got your demmed necklace."

"Watch your mouth, Fitz!"

"That's what you called it, Papa. You said 'demmed necklace.' I heard you."

"And that is exactly what I think of it. But the question is, did you take it?"

"No. What would I want with a stupid necklace? Necklaces are for girls."

"Well, that's settled." Chalgrove gave his sister a quelling look. "Fitz didn't take it. The servants didn't take it. Now, before you start accusing the rest of us one by one, could we, for God's sake, eat? Me stomach's been rumbling for the last half-hour, which is about the length of time Johns has been waiting to announce dinner."

The butler cleared his throat and stepped into the room on cue. "Dinner is served."

"Well, I certainly cannot eat a bite," Mrs. Fielding announced. "I am going to my bed."

"And while you are there look under your pillow," her brother retorted. "You'll probably find your curst diamonds right where you put them for safekeeping."

Mrs. Fielding did not deign to answer and the lethal look she shot Chalgrove was entirely wasted, for he was engaged in hoisting his son to his shoulders for the trip to the dining chamber.

Dinner was a dismal affair. Only Chalgrove, who seemed elated with his victory over an older sister who had intimidated him all during his childhood, ate with a hearty appetite. Fitz was equally unperturbed by the recent drama, but since he had consumed a quantity of chocolates before coming to the table, he was more engrossed in making a fort of his mashed turnips and flipping peas over its walls than with eating.

Sporadic attempts at conversation soon died. Regina's first contribution came at the end of the meal. "I must see how Mother is faring."

"I will go with you." Her fiancé excused himself and followed.

Anne volunteered to put Fitz to bed and then join Audrey in the withdrawing room.

"Well, now, if you coves will pardon me," Chalgrove said to the remaining two gentlemen at the table, "I think I'll go have me glass with the old man before he retires. He'll want to know what's going on under his roof. Though come to think on it, I'll bet a monkey he already knows. For an invalid who scarcely ever leaves his bedchamber, the old devil don't miss much, and that's the gospel truth."

"Well, now, big brother," Larry remarked a few moments later, "seems you and I are the sole survivors." He raised his crystal goblet. "Here's to the country. And we thought it would be dull." He took a long draft of claret before he noticed that his brother had not joined him but was twisting his glass in his hands, staring down at its contents. "Don't look so glum, old fellow. I am sure this is merely another tempest in a teacup. I can tell you this. As much as it pains me to lose Regina, I do not envy Lord Elliott his mama-in-law. She does like to send up an atmosphere. And I am sure Chalgrove has the right of it. She will no doubt find the 'demmed necklace' right where she put it for safekeeping."

"No, I do not think so," Lord Hunt said slowly.

"You don't? Why ever not?"

"Because I greatly fear that Audrey took it."

There was a moment's silence while Larry stared at his twin in disbelief.

"You fear *what*?"

"You heard me."

"I could not have done. You cannot actually believe that our Audrey would take her sister's necklace. Why, I've half a mind to draw your cork. I would, by Jove, if I weren't convinced you're a hopeless Bedlamite and not responsible for thinking such a thing."

"I know." Danforth looked miserable, unable to meet his brother's eyes. "It is hard to believe. But you don't understand. Audrey is desperate. She owes the cent-per-centers two thousand pounds."

"She what?"

"You heard me."

"Then why the devil don't you pay them? My God, Danforth, don't tell me *you* are up the River Tick."

"No, certainly not. In fact, I did pay them."

"Then why the deuce are you flinging about these mad accusations?"

"Because Audrey doesn't know I paid off her debt. She thinks I know nothing about it."

"And you kept her in ignorance?" Larry was looking at his brother as though he had never seen him before.

"I know it sounds hard-hearted, but—"

"It *is* hard-hearted."

"Dammit, let me explain. I did it for the best. You see, she lost the money gambling. And you know all about the Broughams and gambling. It is practically a disease with them. You remember Papa telling us that Sir Jervis nearly ruined himself at faro. And how Chalgrove had to leave the country because of his gaming debts. Papa was very proud of Audrey because she would hardly ever agree even to play for fish. So when her creditors came knocking at my door and I learned what she had done, well, I paid them off. But I decided not to tell her. I thought that if it was bad blood, well, perhaps suffering the consequences would make her think twice before she got into the same sort of coil again."

"Well, you damn well better tell her immediately."

"I can't do that. She did not wish me to know."

"Being in your black books is preferable to resorting to thievery, wouldn't you say? Not that I believe for a minute that Audrey would have taken that blasted necklace. She could have helped herself to the Hunt jewels at any time."

"She wouldn't do that and you know it. They are in trust, not to go out of the family."

"But she would pocket her sister's necklace without a qualm?" Larry looked scornful.

"That is exactly the point. You heard her. She

109

does not believe that Mrs. Fielding has any more right to the thing than she has."

"Perhaps you're right," Larry agreed reluctantly. "I did realize that Audrey was disturbed about something. And I think you were a scoundrel not to tell her that you had paid her debt. Now you have no choice. Go tell her. Then if she did take the thing, she can sneak it back."

"And she'll know that we know she is not only a gambler but a thief as well. That should do wonders for our relationship." Danforth's voice was bitter.

"Right." Larry looked ill. "But what choice have we?"

There was a bleak silence.

"Perhaps we could find the necklace and return it."

"Even given the unlikely possibility that we could find it, if she's as desperate as you say, she might just turn around and nick the family silver."

"That won't be necessary." Lord Hunt went on to tell his brother about the beautiful matched pearls "they" were giving their stepmother for Christmas. "The pearls will be worth more than enough to cover her debt. And I've had a word with the pawnbroker. He will return them to me immediately after she pawns them."

"And then we just fail to notice that she never wears them?" Larry scoffed.

"That's right. Oh, damn it all, I can't think of everything. Audrey will probably have a fake replacement made and that's what we won't notice. The thing is, we have got to find that confounded necklace before someone else spots it among her things. We've no time to waste. They'll soon be taking in the tea board." He jumped up from the table and his brother followed.

Their search was hampered by the need to leave Audrey's things apparently undisturbed and by the necessity of keeping their ears cocked for the sound of footsteps. They were thwarted in the latter instance when Larry, who had crawled beneath the bed, called for Danforth to "hold the candle, for God's sake, where a cove could see." Danforth obliged by squirming, taper in hand, halfway beneath the four-poster to light up the recesses. When the chamber door opened, the dust ruffle muffled its sound.

"Just what, exactly, are you two doing?"

The twins looked back over their shoulders to observe their stepmama, on hands and knees, staring at them. Her expression was not cordial.

Chapter
Fifteen

CAPTAIN HUNT STRETCHED HIMSELF OUT ON THE BED and sighed. It would be an exaggeration, he thought, to consider this the worst day of his life. After all, it had some pretty stiff competition. The battle of Waterloo sprang instantly to mind, only to be overset by the ringing slap Regina had administered as he stood shivering by the bonfire. But the look on Audrey's face when he and Danforth had been caught red-handed ... well, that easily ranked high.

He had, he recollected, thought with commendable speed. "I say," he had said after they crawled out from underneath her bed and he stood dusting off his evening smalls nonchalantly, "have you by chance seen my signet ring? I've somehow lost it."

"How odd. Perhaps it ran away with Judith's diamonds." Audrey's voice had been more frigid than the pond water.

He had laughed, but not too convincingly he

feared. "I think not. It's of no particular value, but I am attached to it. We have turned our own room upside down." Danforth had been of no help, blast him, looking down at the floor, unable to meet Audrey's accusing eyes. "Then I recalled that the last time I was in here I kept pulling it on and off, remember?" She had shown no recollection of a business that had never happened, but still he had forged ahead. "Anyhow, I thought it might have rolled underneath the bed. But apparently not."

Whether Audrey had been convinced by his Banbury tale remained a mystery. But looking back now on the harrowing experience, he believed that she had thawed a bit. Still, that might be mere wishful thinking on his part. He sighed again, glanced at his black evening slippers resting on the snowy counterpane, and kicked them off. He poured himself a glass of claret from the decanter he had thoughtfully provided, then lit a cheroot. As he sank back again against the headboard and blew out a cloud of smoke, he sighed for a third and final time.

Whether due to the claret or the cigar, his natural optimism was beginning to reassert itself. Yes, by George, he told himself as he puffed away, Audrey had to have been convinced by the explanation. Hadn't that ungrateful mute, Danforth, congratulated him, once they were out of earshot, on his cool head and quick thinking under fire?

As she left her mother's chamber, Regina, too, was looking forward to her bed. Not that she expected to sleep. That comfort had been in short supply of late. But an absorbing novel waited on her bedside table along with an inexhaustible supply of candles. She would read the whole night through if need be.

It had finally taken a generous draft of laudanum to calm her mother. Even Lord Elliott's reassurance that the necklace was bound to resurface had failed to soothe her. "If one of the servants did take it," he had pointed out reasonably, "they will return it now the hue and cry is on. They won't risk possible discovery."

"What risk?" her mother had wailed. "That upstart will not allow them to be searched."

"You can speak to Sir Jervis about it in the morning," Elliott had told her.

"He is entirely under That Person's thumb."

And so it had gone until the laudanum had finally taken effect.

As she reached for her chamber doorknob, Regina's eyes misted at the memory of Elliott's unflagging patience. She did admire him so. Was it true what they said, that such feelings were the best basis for marriage and could in time turn into romantic love? Her sigh was heartrending as she stepped inside the room. It quickly converted itself into a gasp. "You!" she exclaimed.

Lawrence was stretched out upon her bed, reading her book and smoking a cheroot.

"Well, finally. You certainly took your time. Was afraid I might fall asleep. Can't say this book has been much help." He turned the volume around to squint through the smoke at its cover. *Roderick Random.* "Regular soporific, I'd call it. Or maybe that's the idea. Having trouble sleeping, are you? Guilty conscience perhaps. Marrying a man for his title and fortune can have that effect, so they tell me."

She strode purposefully to the bed and yanked the book out of his hand. "Get out!"

"Now don't fly off into the boughs."

"How dare you! What makes you think you can

invade my bedchamber whenever the notion strikes you?"

"How else am I going to get the chance to talk to you?" he asked reasonably, sinking back against the pillows and preparing for a chat. "You seem to stay in Elliott's pocket. You know, I've wondered about that, actually. Is it to be with him or to avoid me?"

"One does tend to spend time with one's fiancé. That is, I collect, the purpose of an engagement period."

"Ah, yes. So I recall."

"Indeed? You were betrothed, were you? I presume the poor girl came to her senses."

"That's a cruel way to put it. But you should know."

"I? I hope you are not implying that *we* were ever betrothed."

"Well, I believed so. There were certain words spoken. You really cannot have forgot." He glared accusingly.

"All I can recall is that you ran off to join the army. Where you heroically lost an eye and the use of a limb."

"Ah, yes, that. That is what I wanted to explain. But I do wish you would sit down and not loom over me like a vengeful goddess." He took a deep swallow of wine. "Won't you please pull up a chair and join me? Pray take note that I do not ask you to share the bed."

"You are foxed," she pronounced.

"No, not really. Slightly disguised, merely. It's been a harrowing evening. Speaking of which, how is your dear mother?"

"Prostrated. As anyone would be who had lost a piece of jewelry worth a fortune."

"Upset you, too, has it? As the only daughter—

only *child*, to be more exact—it would have eventually come to you. Still, though, I collect that Lord Elliott can keep you well supplied with trinkets. A diamond a day, no doubt, with extras thrown in for birthdays and Christmas."

"Will you please leave?"

"No, dammit. Not till I have explained myself."

"Explain yourself? That would take more time than one's allotted three score years and ten."

"You are hard, you know. It would serve you right if I didn't explain."

"There is no need for tedious explanations. You wished to make a complete fool of me. It worked admirably."

"Well, if I'm not allowed to explain, I will apologize. The eye patch and limp were a blatant attempt to work on your sympathies. Oh, I beg pardon. There I go again, breaking your rules. The thing is, it's hard to do a proper apology without explanations. But be that as it may, I practiced a most unworthy deception of which I am totally ashamed. Except . . . it did work there for a minute, didn't it?"

She gave him a withering look.

"Well, perhaps not." He took another generous draft of claret.

"Don't you think you have had quite enough of that?"

"Oh, no. Not nearly enough. It appears that I can't stop playing 'what if' in my mind." He paused expectantly. "You are supposed to ask 'What if what?' "

"I am not even slightly interested in your musings."

"Oh, you have made that quite clear. You are at pains to avoid all philosophical musings. But personally I cannot help wondering how things would have turned out had I not gone away."

"Pray don't confuse idle speculation with philosophy."

"And don't you call it *idle*. That sounds leisurely. And my speculation is damned hard work, I can assure you."

"Then go to bed. Your own bed, that is, and sleep it off."

"I don't wish to. Danforth is in my bed and he snores. How many bedchambers would you say there are in this mausoleum?"

"I neither know nor care."

"Well, certainly enough to give my brother and me separate rooms. But that old skinflint doesn't want to make up extra fires.

"Well, never mind that. I was wondering whether everything would have changed anyway if I had stayed at home." He held up a hand to stop her retort. "I am not just talking about you and me. Even if I had camped on your doorstep, your mother would have seen to it that you made a 'good' marriage, dutiful daughter that you are. The change in you is worst of all, of course. But, trust me, the business doesn't stop there. Audrey's your aunt, is she not?"

"You are just now discovering that?"

"You two are close, isn't that so? Everyone says you look like Audrey, though I can't see it. Of course you both are beauties. But that would not guarantee closeness. Could work just the opposite, in fact."

"Is there a point to this rambling?"

"Well, yes. I am about to ask if you have noticed a change in Audrey."

"I cannot say that I have." What she also could

not say was that his return had made her oblivious to all else around her.

"Well, you should have noticed. Audrey is not happy."

"She is older now. It is natural for her to be more serious."

"She is the same age as your fiancé. A bit younger, actually."

"Do not start that again."

"Sorry. But whether you've noticed it or not, Audrey has changed. And I wonder if I might have prevented—certain things—if I had stayed at home."

"As usual, you give yourself too much credit."

"Perhaps you're right. And then there's Danforth. He was always shy, you know. Especially with the ladies. Always depended on me in that area."

"And you were quick to oblige."

He frowned reproachfully. "For his sake only. But lately he has grown, well, 'holier-than-thou' I believe one might call it. I can't tell you in just what way, but if I could tell you, you would agree with me. No, I should not have left home," he said sadly. But then he rallied. "That's balderdash. I had to go."

"Had to?" Her look was scornful.

"Yes, had to. You never did understand that, did you?"

"How could I? You left without bothering to explain."

"I know. That was cowardly. But I couldn't face you. The truth is, if you had begged me to stay, I would have and I could not. Not being a man, thank God, I doubt you can understand that."

"I collect you are going to speak of duty . . . patriotism."

"No. Well, yes, in part. All those other coves were

getting shot and slashed for king and country and I could see no reason for me to be an exception. I am, after all, a second son. That kind of thing is expected of our lot. But that was not the real reason I went."

"Very well. I will play your game. What was the real reason? Adventure?"

"Adventure?" He mulled over the word. "I think battle's only an adventure to someone who has never been in one. 'Hell' is a better term. The honest truth is, I had to see if I was up to that sort of business. Had the bottom for it. If I had chosen to stay at home, well, I would have always wondered if I'd merely funked it.

"But enough of this." He gave himself a shake. "I am getting morbid. Which is totally inappropriate. For after all this is the Christmas season. The season to be jolly, as they say. Which brings me to another reason why I was waiting for you. I have something to show you, Gina love." He began fishing underneath the pillow and after a bit of a search pulled out a very bedraggled piece of plant life. He held it up triumphantly.

"You wished me to see *that*?" She stared uncomprehendingly.

"It's mistletoe, you clodpole! To jolly up the season. Had to go down to the servants' hall to find some. All Fitz and Danforth fetched home were boughs of holly. Disgusting. I don't give a fig what the song says, you can't jolly up the season with just boughs of holly. It takes this little shrub to put some life into the festivities." He waved the sprig for emphasis. Three white berries promptly fell off it.

"I hope you don't intend . . ." Regina was backing away as he sat upright and swung his legs off her bed.

"Of course I do. But no need to look so alarmed. There is nothing at all improper in it. In fact, under the rules of Christmas it is mandatory. Everybody kisses everybody beneath the mistletoe."

"Not at midnight. And in a lady's chamber."

"They do if that's where they and the mistletoe happen to be."

Regina had backed away, only to come to rest against an unyielding wall. She considered calling for help, but the ensuing embarrassment (not to mention what her mother would say) would be far worse than the ritual of the mistletoe. Regina closed her eyes and thought of England.

Lawrence's lips met her own, lightly at first, then warming rapidly to their work, melting all her virginal determination to remain detached. The warm glow suffused her, first weakening her knees, then, not content with just that debility, surging onward to leave her whole body limp. She made one last desperate effort at aloofness, but to no avail. The music was far too powerful to resist. For somewhere in the recesses of her mind, noisy carolers clutching sprigs of mistletoe were singing: Fa, la, la, la, la, la, la, la, la.

Chapter Sixteen

SIR JERVIS'S MASTER PLAN DID NOT APPEAR TO BE working. It was up to him to give matters a helpful push. After finishing a hearty breakfast, he sent his valet to fetch his son.

Chalgrove was, as ever, cheerful. "Well, you are looking fit, sir," he remarked as he took a seat beside his father's bed. His eyes strayed to the beef bones heaped upon the plate. "Seem to have enjoyed your breakfast."

Sir Jervis's scowl was awful to behold. "*Fit*, you call it. Just because a cove gnaws a few bones to keep the grim reaper away through Christmas, you dare to call it *fit?*"

"No need to get on your high horse. I was simply trying to look on the bright side."

"Humph." It had occurred to Sir Jervis that it did not serve his purpose to be at daggers drawn. "Well, didn't mean to bite your head off," he muttered.

This came the closest to an apology that Chalgrove had ever heard his parent make. He shifted uneasily in his chair. Maybe the old terror actually was dying.

Sir Jervis, unaware of his son's reaction, forged ahead. "Called you here to ask a favor. Want you to drive Anne to the village."

"You want me to drive Miss Welbourne?" Chalgrove was more confused than ever about his parent's mental state. "Don't you have a coachman for that sort of thing?"

"Joe's laid up with lumbago," Sir Jervis improvised. "Besides, thought you'd like to visit your old haunts again."

"Well, that does sound like a prime notion. Except for the fact that I couldn't take Miss Welbourne to any of 'em."

"I did not mean *those* old haunts," his father snapped. "Thought you should give the respectable village folk a chance to see you. Ain't as if you've got anything better to do, have you?"

"No, no. Glad to oblige. When do we go?"

"Soon as you find Anne and give her this." Sir Jervis shoved a list of quite unnecessary errands toward him. "Tell her I want you to go right away."

Once Chalgrove had left the room, Sir Jervis groaned heavily. "Head thick as a Yule log," he muttered to himself. "Both girls always had more in the brain pan. Still, Anne's bright as a pin. She can run things and he'll never know it."

The Hunt twins were the sole occupants of the withdrawing room. Danforth was hunkered over a chessboard trying to concentrate. Lawrence was more actively engaged. The former jumped when the latter dropped a hammer.

"What in God's name are you doing?"

"Decorating. Decking the halls."

"There are servants for that sort of thing, you know."

"Ah, but this requires an expert. It is all a matter of proper deployment, you see."

"What are you raving on about?" Danforth lifted his eyes from the chessboard and glanced around. "Haven't you noticed that this place already looks like Birnam Wood? Thanks to young Fitz, Miss Welbourne, and myself."

"Oh, yes, I have noticed. And a pathetic job you three made of it. Now I can understand the oversight of an infant. And Miss Welbourne's modesty would prevent her from remarking on the oversight. But you, big brother, have no excuse. You are, in fact, pathetic. And I am doing this for you, actually."

"Decorating for me? Well, save yourself the trouble. I think things look sufficiently festive as they are."

"You really are a nodcock, Dan. You haven't the slightest—" He was interrupted by Chalgrove, who poked his head inside the door.

"I say. Have you two coves seen Miss Welbourne this morning?"

"No, sorry," Lawrence said, while at the same time his twin answered, "She's sewing in the morning room."

"Fancy you knowing that," Lawrence commented with a smirk.

"Oh, thanks. I'll just ... Ah, here she comes."

The twins heard Chalgrove greet Anne and convey Sir Jervis's plan for their morning. Danforth looked thunderous. He waited until the two had left the hall, then gave the chess pieces an impatient swipe and hurried toward the door.

"I say, where are you off to?"

"To find young Fitz."

"Fitz? Whatever for?"

"He won't want to miss an outing to the village."

"Oh, I see." His brother laughed. "You're providing a chaperon."

"You could say so."

"I do say so. Regular little Machiavelli, ain't you?"

He chuckled even more as he listened to Danforth race up the stairs.

In spite of his efforts, Lawrence was afraid to hope that the coming evening would be any less of a disaster than the previous one. Certainly the pall of gloom had not lifted from Stonebridge Park during the day. Mrs. Fielding was still suffering the loss of her necklace and incensed over the fact that her father (influenced by Anne, she had no doubt) would not order a proper search. Audrey had been noticeably distant in her dealings with his brother and himself. He feared that she had not fully accepted his signet-ring story and suspected their true motive for searching her chamber. As for Regina—Well, it was best not to dwell on Regina. She seemed determined to pretend that the night before had never happened, hoping, perhaps, that he had been too foxed to recall anything today.

So, all in all, he did not place much faith in his scheme to liven up the house party. Still, when the gentlemen arrived in the withdrawing room ahead of the ladies, he took it as an omen. At least he did until Sir Jervis's valet wheeled the old gentleman into the room.

Then he was hard put to suppress a sigh. The patriarch's presence was sure to be a dampener. Sir Jervis underscored this prediction by responding with frowns and grunts to the greetings of the other men.

Oh, the devil with him, Lawrence resolved silently. Aloud he said, "I say, I think all you gentlemen may wish to stand closer to the doorway." With a mischievous grin he pointed to the clump of mistletoe placed strategically above the entrance.

The sight of the Christmas greenery provoked little enthusiasm—except from Chalgrove, who laughed appreciatively, then paused midchuckle. "That is all very well for you coves, but I am related to all the females here. Of course," he said, brightening, "there is Anne." This afterthought earned him a lethal look from Danforth, who edged closer to the doorway.

"How enterprising of you, Captain," Lord Elliott observed dryly as he, too, moved defensively toward the mistletoe.

"You mean you're supposed to kiss any lady who stands underneath that stuff?" Fitz had just engaged in a whispered conversation with his father. Horror intensified his volume. "Demmed if I will."

"You tell them, lad." Sir Jervis looked at his grandson with near approval. "Damned silly custom."

"Oh, come, sir." The Waterloo veteran displayed his mettle. "Your memory can't be that short."

"My memory's a dashed sight better than yours, young fellow," the octogenarian snapped. "Seems like you've failed to recall that you are obliged to kiss any female who decides to stand underneath that weed. That includes long-in-the-tooth antidotes. Don't tell me you're panting to kiss me starchy daughter Judith."

The soldier shrugged. "If it's the price one has to pay."

"Humph." The old man gave him an appraising look.

Lord Elliott moved a bit closer to the door.

Indeed, of a sudden the gentlemen seemed to be viewing the procedure more as a competition than as an evening's lark. Trying not to make their maneuvering obvious, they jockeyed for position. Danforth was determined to beat Chalgrove off the mark. Lord Elliott would be damned before that military here-and-thereian stole one more march on him. Young Fitz picked up some of his elders' tension but was at a loss to comprehend it. He went to stand by his grandfather's Bath chair, recognizing, in this instance at any rate, a kindred spirit.

He gave the chair an experimental push.

"Stop that, you young rapscallion."

"Can I ride in it?"

"No. Be quiet."

For soft-soled footsteps were heard approaching. The gentlemen held their collective breath. They released it in one silent sigh. Mrs. Fielding stood framed in the doorway.

Her expression did not radiate Christmas cheer. "Dour" would have best described it. She was wearing black crape as though in mourning, which indeed she was. Her dinner gown left throat and bosom starkly bare, lest anyone forget the purloined diamonds.

Sir Jervis broke the silence with a wicked chuckle. "Well, what are you waiting for, Captain? Here's your chance."

But whether from an innate courtesy or from a need to practice his flanking maneuver, it was Lord Elliott who rose to the occasion. The viscount stepped forward and gave his fiancée's mother a chaste kiss upon the cheek.

126

"Good gracious! Whatever . . ." Mrs. Fielding was startled right out of her tragic mode. Then following the gazes of the chuckling men, her eyes traveled upward. "Mistletoe!" She all but leaped out from under it.

Fitz, who had been watching the proceedings with a jaundiced eye, now snickered. "Did you see the old 'un jump?" he asked Sir Jervis.

Anne Welbourne arrived next and paused upon the threshold. Chalgrove Brougham had been keeping a watchful eye on Lord Hunt, his likely rival, preparing to beat him to this quarry. But Chalgrove had reckoned without his lordship's brother. Since he had no prior knowledge of the bond between the twins, the oversight was understandable. But as he lunged toward Anne, Lawrence blocked him just long enough for Danforth to make his move.

The kiss could not, by any stretch of the imagination, have been called "perfunctory." Anne Welbourne emerged from it wild-eyed and gasping. The look she gave her attacker was a blend of astonishment and insight. "Whatever—" she managed to gasp in an unconscious repetition of Mrs. Fielding's sentiments.

Lord Hunt was too shaken to reply. He merely pointed up toward the mistletoe.

"Oh, I see." Her cheeks flamed red as she fled the danger.

Lord Elliott had, with narrowed eyes, observed the cooperative maneuver of the twins and was determined not to be outflanked. So when he heard female footsteps hurrying toward them, he was on his toes and ready. Perhaps he failed to notice that it was Audrey and not Regina who paused beneath the mistletoe, giving a puzzled look at the collected gentlemen. Be that as it may, he acted.

The old Christmas custom seemed to be taking on a brand-new dimension. Perhaps Lord Hunt had set the tone with his performance. If so, Lord Elliott now raised it several notches. As the kiss went on, the others hardly knew which way to look. Chalgrove finally went so far as to clear his throat noisily, either from embarrassment or as a warning.

For Regina had arrived and was standing beside the oblivious couple, still locked in each other's arms. Her face gave no indication of her thoughts. Her eyes did travel upward, though, to spy the mistletoe.

"My, that does look like fun." She broke into the charged silence that followed the conclusion of the kiss. As Audrey struggled for composure and backed away, her niece stepped deliberately into her abandoned spot. Lord Elliott's reaction time was slow. Embarrassingly slow. He appeared dazed. Disoriented. Then suddenly he snapped to, gave an awkward laugh, and bussed his fiancée perfunctorily upon the lips.

"Well, is that business finally over?" Fitz inquired. "That's all the females, ain't it? They're nothing but a bunch of widgeons if you ask me, getting caught out that way."

"Oh, you think so, do you?" Regina tried to restore some normalcy to a situation that clearly had got out of hand. She strolled casually over to young Fitz, still standing by his grandfather's chair, and before he could guess her intent, stooped and kissed him with a resounding smack.

"Hey, watch it!" Fitz protested, wiping his lips vigorously but looking not nearly so displeased as he might have wished to be. "No fair!"

"Widgeon!" Regina taunted, and pointed directly

overhead to a sprig of mistletoe dangling from the chandelier.

"The demmed stuff's everywhere!" Fitz exclaimed.

"Language, boy!" His father spoke more from habit than from hope.

"And a Happy Christmas to you, Grandfather." Regina gave the wheelchair a nudge that centered it directly underneath the dangling greenery and kissed him affectionately.

"Harrumph!" was his reaction. But he, too, was not displeased by his inclusion.

The company went into dinner in an almost festive mood. Fitz paused a moment by the sideboard. It was undoubtedly the lavish display of sweets he saw there that caused him to look so pleased as he took his seat, elevated by Dr. Johnson's dictionary, at the table.

Conversation flowed. It was as if the diners wished to postpone any reflection on the strange effects of dangling mistletoe. Audrey, in particular, was almost feverish in her gaiety, recalling pranks that she and Chalgrove had played upon their governesses when they were children, then laughing inordinately as her brother added his own recollections. Mrs. Fielding participated by correcting their faulty memories and Lawrence chimed in by relating a few hair-raising tales of the childhood mischief he and his twin brother had got into.

"What Larry should say is the mischief *he* got us into. I was always the innocent party." Danforth endeavored to look virtuous and everybody laughed.

"Actually, he is not funning. What he says is all too painfully true."

Regina's dampening tone produced a momentary silence.

Chalgrove broke it. "I hope you have not been listening to any of this, Fitz," he said mock seriously. "Your elders should be setting you a better example."

"Listening to what, Papa?" The child's head, which had been nodding perilously close to his plate, jerked upright. Everyone laughed again and the gaiety was restored.

The only one immune to the festive mood was Sir Jervis. He sat at the head of his table, eating very little but observing everything from beneath his bushy brows. His gaze moved speculatively from his second daughter to Lord Elliott, then to his granddaughter and on to Lawrence Hunt. After failing to solve this particular conundrum, his eyes refocused on his son, who seemed far more interested in his oyster patties than in Anne Welbourne seated beside him. He looked next from Anne to Lord Hunt. They seemed determined not to look at each other. He frowned reflectively.

At the final remove young Fitz roused himself. "Is it time for pudding?"

A liveried footman was placing a domed dish upon the table. He removed the silver cover with a flourish to expose a steaming, holly-garnished Christmas pudding. And something else.

A startled mouse stopped nibbling at the confection, looked about him with frightened beady eyes, then bolted. He ran the full length of the table while the ladies shrieked, wineglasses toppled, and chairs scraped hastily backward.

The horrified footman lunged for the rodent, trying to trap it beneath the silver lid. He only succeeded in reversing the mouse's course, sending it scampering back up the mahogany table to the accompaniment of the same, though now heightened, mass confusion. The thoroughly panicked mouse at last made a suicidal leap off the table and was pursued out of the room by the flustered footman.

The diners resumed their places. There was a moment's silence as all eyes turned toward Fitz. The lad contrived to look particularly innocent, quite angelic, in point of fact.

And then, suddenly, the silence was broken by a strange, eerie sound, almost as startling as a mouse served up in a silver dish. It began as a low, preliminary rumble, in the manner of distant, barely discerned thunder. Then it slowly increased in volume, sputtering and coughing like one of Mr. Trevithick's lately invented engines. All eyes left young Fitz and settled in unison on Sir Jervis. There was a ghastly moment when it was feared that the old man was suffering a seizure. But then it slowly dawned on the assembled company that what they were actually hearing was the sound of Sir Jervis, laughing.

Chapter
Seventeen

AFTER SIR JERVIS HAD BEEN WHEELED FROM THE TAble still wheezing with mirth, the diners were left with the remainder of the evening to cope with. For Mrs. Fielding this was no problem. She informed them icily that she had developed a splitting headache and wished to retire immediately. Perhaps it was the absence of reaction to this declaration that caused her to enlarge upon it. "I am totally unaccustomed to having my dinner interrupted in such a fashion. My physician keeps saying that a delicate system—and he has never known one, he says, as delicate as mine—requires peace and harmony. And at no time more so than at meals. And why anyone—*anyone*—would allow a child to dine with adults is beyond my understanding."

"Now look here, Judith." Chalgrove sprang to his cub's defense. "Fitz behaved himself admirably, b'gad. Never heard a peep out of him."

"Behaved admirably, brother? You call introducing a mouse to the table *admirable*?"

"Fitz had nothing to do with that mouse!"

"Oh, no?" Her look was eloquent. Fitz kept his eyes glued on his plate.

It was obvious that the seeds of suspicion had been planted. Chalgrove glanced uneasily at his far-too-engrossed child. But having engaged in battle, he soldiered on. "That ain't the first mouse that ever invaded Stonebridge, as you must know."

"It was the first ever to be served up in style at dinner."

Lawrence tried, not quite successfully, to turn a laugh into a cough. It was infectious. First Regina giggled, then there was smothered laughter all around.

"I am glad you are all able to find the incident amusing." Mrs. Fielding gave the company a censorious look as she pushed back her chair and rose to her feet. "I, for one, find such conduct reprehensible."

"Oh, really, Mother. I am sure Uncle Chalgrove is right. The mouse must have got into the pudding while in the kitchen."

"Believe what you will. I will bid you all good night." Mrs. Fielding swept from the room with injured dignity.

Regina's brief moment of levity passed quickly. "Like mother, like daughter," the uncharitable might have thought. For once the company had reassembled in the withdrawing room, she sent up a signal of unsociability by settling down at the pianoforte to play soft, melancholy tunes. Her fiancé felt duty-bound to join her. But since there were no pages to turn and no welcoming smile, it was with a measure of relief that he accepted Chalgrove's invitation for a game of whist.

Anne and Audrey were persuaded to join them. As soon as they were seated, Chalgrove began to shuffle the cards with a flourish and a flair that caused the eyes of the other players to widen.

Danforth, in the meantime, had picked up the book someone had abandoned on a reading table. He then positioned his chair with more regard for a view of the whist players than for candlelight on the printed page.

Lawrence, after a pensive look in the direction of the pianoforte (duly noted by the player of that instrument), strolled over to join young Fitz. The lad was seated before the more distant of the two fireplaces, pouring colored sticks out of a wooden box. "Hmmm," Lawrence mused as he stood looking down at the tumbled pile. "Looks impossible. The trick, as I recall it, is to pour 'em out from a greater height so that they will scatter."

"If you do that you might as well not play at all" was the scornful answer. "There'd be no point in it."

"True," the captain conceded.

"Might as well just lay 'em out one by one. Two inches apart."

"I stand corrected."

"Want to play?"

"Don't mind if I do." Lawrence sank to the floor. "You first. I've forgotten the proper technique. Been years since I've played spillikins, you see."

"Like this." With fierce concentration aided by his tongue between his teeth, Fitz delicately applied the sharpened point of a white stick to the side of a yellow one. A purple, resting underneath it, moved.

"Damnation!"

"Tough luck, old boy. My turn, I believe."

* * *

The first rubber of the whist game had been hard-fought, with Elliott and Audrey barely eking out a win.

"We'll get them this time, Anne." As Chalgrove spoke, the shuffled cards arced in a stream from one hand to the other. "What say we make things a bit more interesting?"

"What do you mean?" Audrey had gone a trifle pale.

"Why, a wager, of course."

"No!"

Her voice was so vehement that it caused all heads in the drawing room to turn her way and made Fitz jostle a stick. "No fair!" he wailed.

"I agree. Take another turn." Lawrence spoke automatically as he watched the whist table uneasily.

Audrey, obviously, was agitated. Her brother, just as obviously, was offended. "No need to fly off into the boughs," he said. "I was not about to suggest playing for pound points. Just some small flutter—a farthing will do—to add a bit of excitement to the game."

"I cannot understand that attitude." Audrey's voice was shaky. Anne and Elliott studied their cards intently. "A game should be played for its own sake entirely. I do not understand this compulsion to introduce wagering into a mere pastime."

Chalgrove threw down the hand he had just dealt and rose to his feet in a fury. "And I cannot understand your priggish attitude. My God, Audrey, you are worse than Judith. Is it some family sickness that requires everyone to view the most paltry wager as a leap into hellfire?"

"Hellfire has nothing to say in the matter. It is just that—"

"Spare me," he interrupted. "I know what you are about to say. It ain't gambling in general that you object to. It is gambling and Chalgrove. Well, I have heard it all before. And in this very house. So I'll not stay for your prosy lecture but bid all of you good night."

He stormed from the room as shocked eyes followed his exit. Young Fitz took advantage of this distraction to surreptitiously rearrange the pile of sticks to his advantage.

"My turn," he said as soon as the door had closed behind his father.

"May I watch?" Anne had excused herself from the whist table to come stand over them.

"Better still, join us," Lawrence invited. "The more the merrier. This little Jack Sharp is beating me unmercifully." His eyes narrowed as he surveyed the rearranged pile. "By fair means or foul."

"I don't know what you're on about," Fitz said virtuously as he deftly extracted six sticks from the grouping.

"Are you quite all right?" Elliott looked anxiously across the table at his partner.

"Y-yes. I do beg pardon. I should not have caused that scene."

"Perhaps not. But given your brother's history, your reaction is understandable."

"But that is where you—and he—mistake the matter." Much to Elliott's alarm, tears were forming in her eyes. "It was not Chalgrove's history I was reacting to. It was my own."

"I think you had best tell me," he said softly after looking around the room. "No one is paying us the slightest bit of notice."

He spoke accurately. Danforth, for whatever reason, had put down his book to join the spillikins game. And as the competition became boisterous,

Regina felt compelled to stop her playing and move close enough to watch.

Lord Elliott dealt out a hand. "We might as well pretend to play. Now tell me what is bothering you."

"I don't think I can. I can't bear for you to think ill of me."

The memory of the mistletoe was foremost in both their minds.

"I don't think that is possible," he said softly.

"I wish that were true." She smiled a wistful smile. "But you speak prematurely." She took a deep breath and poured out the story of her disastrous foray into gambling.

Then quailed before his look of fury. "That type of hell should be shut down by law. God knows how many innocents they have ruined."

"Don't you mean 'fools'?"

"No. Innocents. It is one thing to go to a known gaming parlor, but these private houses that pass their operations off as normal social evenings are, in my opinion, criminal."

"Oh, I agree. But the fact remains that only a complete flat would—"

"But that is what they rely on, don't you see. Getting the innocents into dun territory before they realize what is happening."

She winced. "There you go with that word again. I am too old, Edwin, to be an innocent."

"I know exactly how old you are and I stand by the term." He picked up the unplayed cards and reshuffled them. "But the reason for your predicament is no longer the point. What I do not understand is why Lord Hunt has not paid off the cent-per-centers."

"Because I have not told him." She looked horrified at the very thought of doing so.

"But, my dear, even a prosy lecture on the evils of gambling would be preferable to the strain you have been under."

"Danforth would never scold. He would simply pay my debt."

"Well, then. I must say that I cannot see the problem."

"The problem is, I cannot allow him to discover what I have done. He has just poured the bulk of his capital back into the estate, trying to rectify the years of neglect that happened between his father's death and his majority. He's very keen, too, to acquire more land and employ the new methods of agriculture. And now that Lawrence has sold out, Danforth will wish to establish him. No, I could not trouble him at this time. And besides—" She choked suddenly.

"Yes, besides?"

"I do not expect you to understand this, but I cannot bear for the twins to know how wickedly foolish I have behaved. You see, I really have been a mother to them."

"I have noticed that they appear to have you on a pedestal. Still, I can't believe they would think any less of you by discovering that you are human. But never mind. It will not be necessary to put my theory to the test. I will give you the money."

"No!"

Though spoken much more softly, the exclamation was just as vehement as the one that had infuriated Chalgrove.

"*Lend* you the money then."

"You know I cannot allow you to do that."

"I do not see why not."

"I think you do." For a moment the air was charged between them. "But please don't concern yourself, Edwin dear. I plan to throw myself on Papa's mercy. He will undoubtedly go through the roof first, but he will finally come about."

Lord Elliott looked skeptical but kept his reservations to himself.

The sound of cheering came from the floor as Fitz successfully picked up the final stick. "Good show!" Lawrence congratulated him. "And you didn't have to resort to any, er, adjustment of the distribution."

"I don't know what you're on about."

"He meant you didn't have to mess about with the sticks first," Danforth explained.

"Course not. That would be against the rules." Fitz's look was virtuous.

"Come join us, Regina," Anne said, beckoning. Regina's chair had gradually edged nearer during the spirited game.

"Don't be foolish, Anne," Lawrence mocked. "Such childishness is beneath Miss Fielding's dignity."

Regina gave him a haughty look and plopped down on the floor next to Anne. Fitz dumped the sticks and started a new game.

Regina groaned as she gingerly applied her stick and the others shifted. Anne fared no better. Then it was Lawrence's turn. With a steady hand he disposed of the entire pile.

"Well, by Jove!" Fitz looked at him admiringly.

"You do have a steady hand, I must say," Anne remarked.

"Especially for a one-eyed invalid," Regina added sweetly.

"But he ain't one-eyed," Fitz informed her helpfully. "That was all a sham."

"Was it really?" Her own eyes widened in mock amazement.

"Down, girl." Lawrence frowned.

"He wasn't wounded at all, in fact." Fitz sounded most dejected.

"Well, now, that is not entirely accurate. See?" Lawrence pointed to the minute scar upon his cheek.

"That's nothing." Fitz was scornful. "I got a worse wound than that gathering holly." He pushed up his sleeve to display a scratch and Regina laughed.

"Oh, for God's sake!" Danforth exploded. "The fact of the matter is, my brother is fortunate to be alive."

"We all know that," Regina replied. "Or we do if he was indeed at Waterloo."

"He *was* there. And he *was* wounded." Danforth spoke through teeth that were clenched in fury. "And he was six weeks in hospital. They did not expect him to live, but he did. Would you care to see his medals?"

"Danforth, be quiet!" his brother snapped. "Now let's play."

"I would," Fitz said excitedly. "I would like it above all things."

"You would like what, brat?"

"Like to see your medals. And do you really have real scars?"

"It's your turn, Fitz." Lawrence sighed.

"Could I see your scars?"

"No."

"Please!"

"You can't expect me to strip, old fellow. Let's play."

"Can I come to your bedchamber then and see them?"

"No." Lawrence picked up the wooden sticks and dropped them. They tumbled into a daunting tangle. He gave Regina an evil leer. "But for you, of course, I shall be glad to display 'em anytime."

140

Chapter Eighteen

A THUD ECHOED THROUGH THE UPSTAIRS HALLWAY. Followed by a screech. "Owwww!"

Captain Hunt, in the process of shaving, jerked and nicked himself. "Damnation!" He put down his razor and hurried out into the hall.

Somehow he was not astonished to find Master Fitz at the source of the disturbance. The boy was sprawled just inside Miss Fielding's chamber. That young lady's bare foot was firmly planted upon his back. His arms and legs thrashed about like the appendages of a pinned bug. "Owwww! Lemme up now, will you?"

Larry stepped inside the room and closed the door to contain the uproar. "What's going on here?" he asked conversationally.

"I caught this little monster with his eye to my keyhole again." Regina punctuated each word with a tap of her foot.

"L-l-l-eave off, w-w-will you?" the captive implored.

"Why don't you beg her pardon nicely?" was the captain's suggestion.

"H-h-how can I?" came the aggrieved reply. "She keeps squashing the breath right out of me body."

"He does have a point, you know." Larry was enjoying his role as arbiter. Perhaps the sight of his love, clad only in a nightgown, with her cap dangling by its ribbons down her back and her hair an attractive tangle, had a great deal to do with that attitude. He dabbed at the remaining shaving soap on his face with the corner of the towel he still held. Obsessed with Regina's dishabille, he was forgetful of the fact that he was shirtless.

"Do let him up, Gina. Somehow it doesn't seem in the spirit of the season to kill the little devil on Christmas Eve."

"It would save him the grief of being hanged later." Miss Fielding's words still had to make their way through clenched teeth, but she went so far as to remove her foot from the back of her captive's short jacket. As she did so she allowed her eyes to stray from this target to the newcomer. They froze. Then widened. Miss Fielding gasped and turned a trifle pale.

Master Fitz, scrambling to his feet, was at first relieved to find that his persecutor had focused on another target, then he was puzzled by it. He followed the direction of her gaze.

"Jiminy!"

There was admiration in the childish voice.

"Danforth told the t-truth, didn't he?" Regina managed to say as she stared at the livid, puckered scar that ran all the way from Larry's shoulder to the left side of his rib cage.

The veteran of the Wellington campaign looked

uncomfortable. "It is a habit of his, you know. Practically reflex, you might even say."

"By Jupiter, they carved you up right proper, didn't they?" Master Brougham did not attempt to conceal his respect for Napoleon's finest. He was circling the captain with a critical eye. "But at least your wounds are all in the front," he was able to observe.

"Well, thank you for that."

"Do be quiet, you little villain. Can't you see they almost killed him?" Tears were forming in Miss Fielding's eyes.

"Here, steady on." Larry reached out toward her, but a glance at Fitz's interested expression changed his mind. "As I said, my brother doesn't lie, but he is prone to exaggeration. I wasn't all that near the Pearly Gates."

Miss Fielding failed to look convinced. She reached out and gently traced the path of the scar with her fingertips, then shuddered. "Does it still hurt?" she whispered.

"Not a bit of it."

Fitz was unimpressed by the tender moment. "What I'm wondering is, just what were you doing while the Frenchies were turning you into mincemeat?"

"Fitzgerald!"

"It's a fair question," the boy said defensively as he edged away from the fury in Miss Fielding's eyes.

"It's a ghoulish question."

"All he has to do is answer it."

"Let's just say that I'm here and that the cove who did this to me isn't. What's more, I think you have changed the subject long enough. The matter at issue here is that you were caught—again—with your eyeball glued to Miss Fielding's keyhole. What do you have to say for yourself, brat?"

"I was just trying to be considerate, that's all."

"Come on." Larry gave the boy a level look. "You'll have to do much better than that."

"It's the truth. I had something famous to tell her, but I had to be sure she was awake first, now, didn't I?"

"Did you ever hear of knocking?"

"And supposing I had and supposing she was still asleep, then where would we be?"

Captain Hunt was clearly at an impasse and in spite of herself Miss Fielding's curiosity got the upper hand. "Just what is this famous news?"

"I was going to tell you about your Christmas present. What Lord Elliott got you, I mean."

"That sort of thing is meant to be a surprise, brat," Larry interposed.

"I know that. But I still think she ought to know what he's getting her in case all she's got for him is fusty old worked slippers or something of that sort that ladies are always making for gentlemen. Because if she has, she is really going to be in the basket. For it's my opinion that worked slippers are a shabby gift anytime, but especially as compared to a diamond necklace."

"Whatever gave you the idea that Lord Elliott is giving me a diamond necklace?"

"Saw it, didn't I? In his clothespress."

There was a pause as it occurred to Master Brougham that a bit more explanation might be called for. "I just happened on it when I was chasing a mouse. It ran inside the press. And I wanted to capture it before it wound up on the dining table and sent your mother into fits again," he offered virtuously. "At any rate that's when I saw the necklace. It's in a pretty box and it sparkles like everything. If you ask me, it makes that thing your mother lost look downright shabby. For this one has a pretty green stone dangling down from it."

"Well, well, well," Captain Hunt said softly. "Diamonds *and* emeralds. Looks as if you'll have quite a jolly Christmas, Regina."

"He probably doesn't know what he's talking about. Elliott may not intend that for me at all."

"Then what's he going to do with it? Wear it himself?"

Master Brougham found the question irresistibly witty. He became convulsed with laughter.

His glee still rang in the captain's ears even after two bedchamber doors had been closed behind him.

By tradition Christmas Eve at Stonebridge Park belonged to the servants. A cold collation had been set out for the family in the dining chamber. They consumed it rather glumly while the sounds of revelry, provided by two fiddlers, a harp, and a mighty bowl of wassail, floated up from belowstairs.

"You would think that they would have some consideration," Mrs. Fielding sniffed as a peal of merriment drifted upward to the diners. "They might recall that their master is on his deathbed."

"Fustian." Chalgrove glanced back for a footman, then helped himself liberally to claret. "The old man's bound to live to be a hundred. Too contrary to die. Besides, he wouldn't begrudge the servants a bit of fun. Never did, you know."

"Can we go down and join in, Papa?" Fitz's face was eager.

Chalgrove looked around the table. "I expect we should look in on them. Papa always did as I recall."

"Yes," Audrey agreed. She had earlier begged her brother's pardon for her outburst and was making every effort to smooth his feathers. "By the same token, I collect we should not stay long. Our presence does tend to have a dampening effect."

"It appears to me that they need some dampening." A roar had just been heard from the nether regions.

"Oh, Mother, don't be such a spoilsport." Miss Fielding gave her parent an exasperated look.

"It does not do to permit one's staff such license."

"Surely on one night of the year it does no harm," Audrey interjected mildly before mother and daughter could lock horns.

"There is never any excuse for lowering one's standards, as well-trained servants know. I am sure Lord Elliott will agree. Your servants do not carry on in this manner at Shadwell Hall, do they, sir?"

Elliott, whose mind had been on other things as he rearranged the contents of his plate, looked up, startled. "I beg your pardon?" he asked blankly.

"Oh, never mind," Audrey interposed. "I am sure we have discussed the servant subject sufficiently. Shall we go put in our appearance now and then allow them to get on with their revels?"

The duty visit was soon accomplished. The group that regathered in the withdrawing room seemed more dampened than exhilarated by the experience.

"In England do you have to be a servant to have a good time, Papa?" Fitz inquired as he threw a raisin from his pocket onto the Yule log and watched it sizzle.

"No, of course not." His father laughed. "Though I must admit that at Stonebridge they do seem to be having the best of it." He eyed Anne speculatively. "We could have our own dance, of course. Nothing to prevent it."

"How?" Danforth had not missed the direction of Chalgrove's gaze. "Do you propose to commandeer the fiddlers from down below?"

"Wouldn't think of doing such a shabby thing. But surely someone here can play the pianoforte for us. God knows Papa spent enough on music masters for my sisters. Regina plays, I know. And I'll wager Anne does, too. All young ladies are obliged to learn, regardless of talent."

"Oh, I know!" Audrey clapped her hands as an idea struck her. "We will learn the waltz. I have been dying to master it. Chalgrove, do you waltz?"

"In Ireland? You must be funning."

"How about you, Edwin?"

"No, I fear that I have not even seen it performed, let alone mastered it."

She turned to Larry. "Then it is up to you to teach us all."

"You mean you know how to waltz?" Regina looked indignant.

"Oh, yes, indeed." He pretended not to notice the indignation. "It is quite the rage on the Continent. In fact, it was the most popular dance at the Duchess of Richmond's famous ball. The one before the battle."

"I am amazed you could manage, with your game leg and all."

"But he didn't have a game leg," Fitz corrected her. "And if he did have one, it would have been after the battle and not before. But his leg and his eye weren't hurt a bit, for the Frenchies stuck him in the shoulder and then carved up his ribs. How could you have forgot so soon?" He shook his head in disbelief. "We were looking at the scars this very morning. Why, you even reached out and touched 'em. I wish I could have. You should see them,

Papa. He looks like he's been sliced up like a joint of beef."

There was an uncomfortable silence. Mrs. Fielding was looking at her daughter and Lord Elliott at his fiancée rather oddly. Her face was brick red.

Chapter Nineteen

"It is nice to know that your stay on the Continent was not a complete waste, Lawrence."

Mrs. Fielding had regained her voice. Her disapproval of her stepnephew was blatantly apparent. "At least you contrived to learn the waltz, it seems."

"And now you must teach it to us," Audrey hastily interposed, rising to her feet.

"Well, I, for one, do not consider it a proper dance for young ladies." Her sister looked around her for allies. She found none.

"My heavens, Judith. It is Christmas Eve. We are *en famille*. There can be no notion of impropriety."

"Stop being such a crosspatch, Judith." Chalgrove jumped to his feet. "I, for one, can hardly wait to learn the waltz. Miss Welbourne, will you join me?"

Out of the corner of her eye Anne saw Danforth scowl. "Perhaps I should play," she offered.

"No, let's let Judith do that," Audrey suggested. "She is the most accomplished. And as she has just pointed out, she does not wish to dance."

Mrs. Fielding hesitated.

"Oh, do play, Mother. Aunt Audrey is right. You do so beautifully."

Somewhat mollified, Mrs. Fielding made her stately way to the pianoforte.

"Very well, Larry." Audrey smiled at her stepson. "I am offering myself for the purpose of demonstration. Will you come show us?"

Captain Hunt first went through the steps, solo and slowly, counting out his one-two-threes with emphasis and twirling with an imaginary partner in his arms. "Very well then," he concluded. "Come on, Audrey. Let's try it together while the others watch. If you will, Mrs. Fielding."

The pianist obligingly struck a chord and the waltz began.

Audrey was a natural dancer, graceful and blessed with rhythm. She was soon twirling in Larry's arms as though she had spent her life in old Vienna. When the music stopped, she clung to her stepson's arm breathlessly. "My, that was exhilarating," she gasped, "but one needs to be in the pink of condition to waltz."

"Come on, the rest of you," the captain commanded. "We'll all try it."

The music began again and the novices took the floor, with the gentlemen muttering the waltz beat aloud as they danced. Their performance left something to be desired. Lord Elliott was stiffly mechanical, managing to keep in step but robbing the dance of all grace and beauty. Chalgrove Brougham had launched himself and his partner like twin projectiles. Anything he lacked in rhythm was more than compensated for in verve. As a result of his exuberance, they managed to stay a beat ahead of the music throughout the duration of the dance.

"Hmmm" was the instructor's comment at its conclusion. "Let's make some adjustments here. Audrey, I think you've mastered the technique sufficiently to help Lord Elliott."

As Audrey went to join her new partner, Regina automatically moved Larry's way, trying to appear indifferent. "Oh, Danforth," the dancing master called, "mustn't be a spectator. Come dance with Regina." Her face flushed at the rebuff, whether real or imagined.

The quality of the dancing quickly improved. Like his brother, Danforth was a natural dancer and, after a few false steps, easily mastered the technique. Under the spell of his partner's encouraging words and smile, Lord Elliott soon relaxed. The couple danced as one, revolving gracefully while the lilting music transported them into their own private world. Only Chalgrove seemed to lag behind. Though he still outdid his fellow waltzers in exhilaration, his proficiency left much to be desired. It was with real gratitude that Anne accepted Danforth's invitation to join him for the next attempt.

For a while Fitz had watched the dancing lesson with interest. But long before the clock on the mantel above the Yule log struck twelve, he was fast asleep. Cries of "Happy Christmas" drifted up from belowstairs and roused him. At the same time Mrs. Fielding rose from the pianoforte, declaring herself exhausted and more than ready for her tea.

"Tea! Blast tea!" Young Fitz came bounding to his feet. "It's time for presents. You said we could have our presents at midnight and it's midnight now." He wheeled on Anne accusingly.

"So it is and so we shall." She smiled. "In the dining chamber."

That room had been transformed in their absence. The servants had taken time out from their own revels long enough to carry out the orders Anne had given them. The sideboard was piled high with refreshments and the dining table was covered with pink linen. Three fir trees in giant pots were spaced out on the cloth, each ablaze with circular tiers of colored candles, red and green and white. And by each plate there was a pile of Christmas gifts.

"Ooooh!" Fitz stood spellbound while the others broke into spontaneous applause. There was a period of confusion before everyone, aided by Anne, found their proper places. Young Fitz, however, had no such difficulty. The array of pennywhistles, jumping jacks, and picture books piled around one plate was a dead giveaway. Before the adults were even seated he was tearing into an enormous box, strewing his environs with swatches of brown paper and bits of string. As he snatched off the box lid he gasped for breath. His eyes grew enormous. "Oh, famous!"

The benign looks of interest on the adults' faces quickly turned to horror when from the recesses of the box he reverently lifted out a bright red drum.

"Oh my God!" Danforth breathed.

"Chalgrove, have you entirely lost your mind?"

Fitz's elder aunt impaled his father with a glare.

Chalgrove threw up his hands defensively. "Don't look at me. I didn't buy that thing."

"Then who on earth—" The rest of Mrs. Fielding's question was drowned out by a spirited, though rhythmless, tattoo.

"Stop it, you little heathen!" His father effectively stifled the drumbeat by snatching away the sticks.

"Do you want to wake up Papa? He'll have your scalp for Christmas. Who did buy him this infernal thing?"

All eyes traveled the perimeter of the table until they came to rest on Captain Hunt. That military gentleman was looking sheepish.

"Mr. Childress in the village shop assured me it was the one thing that Fitz truly wanted," he said defensively.

"Oh, it was." Young Fitz's eyes were aglow. "I like it above all things."

"I might have known," Mrs. Fielding observed to the world at large. "And if he had wanted a pistol, I collect you would have furnished that as well."

"Don't be absurd." The captain's snapped retort did nothing to increase his stock with the mother of the girl he loved. "There is no comparison. Every lad wants a drum at some point in his life."

"And some would follow it anywhere," Miss Fielding remarked to no one in particular.

"Well, it certainly is a lovely drum," Anne interposed diplomatically. "But let me suggest, Fitz, that you only play it out of doors. Because of your grandfather's illness, you understand."

"That's what I meant to do," the boy replied virtuously. "Now ain't anybody else going to open their gifts? I could do a *soft* drumroll for each one," he added hopefully. That suggestion was quickly vetoed.

"Do open mine first," Anne suggested. "They are only tokens, mind you."

The guests quickly complied. The ladies all received netted purses and the gentlemen were given handkerchiefs, each with his initial tamboured in a corner. The majority of the "thank yous" were courteous and sincere. Only Lord Hunt appeared delighted. He examined the delicate embroidery in much the same manner as Fitz had viewed his drum. "Oh, I say. Did you do this yourself?" Anne nodded. "Well, I must say it is the nicest monogram I have ever seen."

This fervor caused his twin to reexamine his own gift. He held the handkerchief up to the candle-light, twisting it in every possible way while squinting intently at the embroidery. "Just what I was going to say myself," he finally concluded. Everyone except his brother laughed.

The guests then began to attack their parcels in earnest. Lord Elliott unwrapped a pair of worked slippers that earned Miss Fielding a disgusted look from Master Fitz. "Tried to warn you, didn't I?" he mouthed. She retaliated by sticking out her tongue in his direction, then smiled sweetly at her fiancé's overly effusive thanks.

In her turn she pulled the paper and string off one of the packages piled before her. It was the book that had gone missing from her nightstand. There was no card, but she had little doubt as to the sender. "Oh, the very thing I wanted," she remarked sweetly. "I have searched everywhere for a copy of *Roderick Random*."

"Oooh!" Audrey had unwrapped one of her parcels and was gazing open-mouthed at an exquisite string of perfectly matched pearls. "Oh, they are lovely." Tears welled up in her eyes, both from relief at the solution to her troubles and from grief at the thought of such a stunning gift winding up in a pawnbroker's case. "Oh, you shouldn't have," she choked, looking mistily at her two stepsons.

"Of course we should have," Danforth said brusquely, and Larry whispered, "Damn right. And not a minute too soon," for his brother's ears alone.

"This could be jewelry, too." Mrs. Fielding had picked up the box on her plate and was shaking it experimentally. "I doubt it can live up to your ladyship's matched pearls, but . . ." There was a quick gasp as the box was opened and she peered inside. "Oh, dear heavens!"

"What is it?" Regina was alarmed by her mother's pallor. "Is something wrong?"

"No. Yes," her parent choked. "It is Mama's diamonds." She removed the heavy necklace from its satin bed and held it up for all to see. The jewels picked up the light from the Christmas candles and outsparkled even those festive decorations. Her face was grim as she glared around the table. "All I have to say is that if this is someone's idea of a jest, it is in the poorest possible taste."

But if any guilt resided behind the blank expressions turned in her direction, it was well concealed.

"I agree, Mother," Regina whispered, "but it is Christmas. Let us just be thankful you have your necklace back.

"Now let's see," she exclaimed in a louder voice, "I wonder what this could be."

She was gazing at the rather large, square box in front of her, the last of her Christmas gifts. It was certainly an odd size for jewelry, but perhaps Elliott was playing a prank, trying to fool her. She tore into the package and removed . . . a muff.

There was a moment's tense silence while she peered inside the box to see if something else was concealed there. There was not. Except for the paper that had been wrapped around the muff, the box was empty.

"Oh, do look, everyone. Isn't it lovely?" Regina smiled falsely and held up the white ermine creation for all to see.

"But that's not—" Fitz began, only to end up with a startled "Ouch!" as Captain Hunt administered a well-placed kick underneath the table.

"What did you do that for?" he demanded of his father.

"Do what?"

"Kick me."

"I did no such thing, though you probably needed it."

"Well, somebody did!" His accusing eyes rested on the captain, who merely shrugged and smiled.

"You still have an unopened gift, Lady Hunt," Anne pointed out after they had all admired one another's presents. Among hers had been a pair of kid gloves, several sizes too large, from Chalgrove and Fitz, and a lovely gold locket with no card enclosed.

"I know." Audrey was looking down at the package, puzzled. "I cannot imagine."

"Looks like another jewelry box," Chalgrove observed.

"Yes, it does." She began to untie the string. "You don't suppose that Papa, after all . . . No, he wouldn't. Oh my! My goodness! Oh, my heavens!"

"What is it?" Fitz demanded, standing up in his chair to look.

"It's . . . it's the most gorgeous thing I have ever seen in my whole life," she whispered.

Carefully, reverently, Audrey removed a diamond choker from the little box and held it up. Below the three strands of diamonds blazed an emerald pendant.

"Why, it's the same necklace—Ow!"

This time there was no mistaking the source of the kick. "Shut up, you little scrub," Larry threatened underneath his breath. He then rose quickly to his feet and raised his glass aloft. "Your attention, please! Let me be the first to wish us all a very Happy Christmas."

"Hear! Hear!" Chalgrove echoed, and the others

murmured, "Happy Christmas," as they, too, raised their glasses.

Larry was possibly the only one to notice that Regina's hand trembled slightly as she did so.

Chapter Twenty

CAPTAIN HUNT SHOT UPRIGHT IN HIS BED. HE WAS groping on the floor beside him for his boots when he recalled that he was not still on the Peninsula.

He'd been dreaming again. He had hoped he'd finally put all the nightmares behind him.

No, by gad. It was not a dream. There it was again, the somewhat muffled but unmistakable beat of a drum.

"What is it?" Danforth's counterpane-muffled voice inquired.

"It's the brat and his infernal drum."

"Well, do something. You're the jingle-brain who gave it to him." Having thus disposed of the problem, Danforth rolled over and began to snore.

When the captain opened his bedchamber door he found Fitz planted firmly in front of it, drumsticks at the ready.

"Don't you dare." The soldier commandeered the

sticks and shook them threateningly at the drummer. "You promised to only beat this thing outside, remember?"

"That's what I mean to do. But I had to wake you up first, didn't I?"

"No, you did not."

"Of course I did. Else there wouldn't be time enough. For Papa says we have to go to church. He says they always used to and that my grandfather wouldn't hear of us not going, which doesn't seem fair since he'll stay in bed like always."

"Well, I assure you I'll be ready for church in good time."

"But you don't understand." Fitz's face began to pucker alarmingly. "I need you now."

Larry relented. Slightly. "What for, brat?"

"You promised to teach me 'Over the Hills and Far Away.'"

"And I will. But it can wait." He made as if to turn back into his chamber, but Fitz grabbed a fistful of his dressing gown. Down the hall another chamber door opened. Regina gave them a hard look, then tiptoed to join them. "What is all this commotion about?" she whispered.

It occurred to Captain Hunt that seeing Miss Fielding in her nightclothes was fast becoming commonplace. Not that familiarity in any way dimmed the pleasure. "See what you've done," he said, frowning at Fitz. "You woke up Miss Fielding."

"I wasn't asleep, actually."

"Indeed?" The captain's eyebrows rose. "Worried about something, are we?"

"Not in the least."

Regina's voice lost none of its assurance with the whisker she'd just told. For in truth she had hardly closed her eyes all night. And when she had finally dropped off, it was to dream of a diamond and emerald necklace that kept mysteriously disappearing.

"And quit changing the subject. Could someone please tell me what this row is all about?"

"As far as I've been able to gather, the brat here wants a drum lesson before church."

"That's just part of it. And not even the most famous part. The thing is, Peter told me that the servants built a slide last night and if we hurry we can use it. We need to go now 'cause it might be melted after church."

The captain was about to tell the lad what he could do with his slide when a good look at the eager face made him hesitate.

"How about your father? Couldn't he take you?"

"Papa would kill me if I woke him."

"And you thought I wouldn't? Oh, well, the devil with it. It *is* Christmas. Just let me get some clothes on. How about you, Regina? Are you game to slide?"

"And freeze to death? Don't be daft. I'm going back to bed."

A few minutes later the captain and the small boy stole from the house, both liberally swathed in greatcoats, gloves, and mufflers. No sooner had the door closed behind them than drumsticks made contact with drum.

"Hey, stop that!"

"We're outside now, ain't we?"

"Well, yes, but let's put a little distance between us and anyone fortunate enough to still be asleep."

They trudged in silence through the park for several moments with the hoarfrost crunching beneath their boots and their breath steaming like a smoker's clouds. "Is this far enough?" Fitz inquired.

"Oh, I suppose so."

"Then teach me."

The captain sighed and gave in, thinking longingly of scalding tea and toasted buns. "Here. Give me the drum."

"But I want to do the cadence."

"First let me show you how."

Young Fitz parted reluctantly with his instrument. The captain adjusted the strap over his shoulder and then beat an experimental tattoo. "Loud, ain't it." He grinned.

"Come on. Stop fooling around. You promised to teach me a real soldier's song."

"Oh, very well."

The captain cleared his throat, then while beating out the rhythm with the sticks sang lustily in a passable baritone, " 'Oh, it's fourteen shillings on the drum—' "

"Why?" Fitz interrupted. "Why'd they put money on the drum? Sounds to me like a daft thing to do."

"It's more or less just a figure of speech. That's what they say when a cove enlists—he takes the king's shilling. Now do you want to learn the song or not?"

"Of course I do."

"Then quit interrupting."

The song rang out again.

> "It's fourteen shillings on the drum
> For those who volunteer to come
> To 'list and fight the foe today
> Over the hills and far away.

> "O'er the hills and o'er the main
> Through Flanders, Portugal and Spain

> King George commands and we obey
> Over the hills and far away."

"Oh, I say, that's a topping song. Now can I try it?"

The drumbeat had not awakened Audrey. Like Regina, she had scarcely closed her eyes throughout the night. And when she had, again as in the case of her niece, diamonds and emeralds danced before them.

There had been much discussion the previous evening about who might have given her a gift worth a small fortune. "There has to be a card," Judith had insisted. But a further examination of the discarded wrapping paper revealed nothing. "But you must have some idea who sent it," her sister probed.

Well, she did have. But the idea was unthinkable, let alone one that could be uttered aloud.

"Oh, it's perfectly obvious, isn't it?" Larry had said carelessly. "Hardcastle, the old skinflint, must be planning to come up to scratch after all these years. God knows it's time he got himself leg-shackled. I don't doubt he'll go down on one knee the minute you get back to London. To protect his investment." Everyone had laughed obligingly.

For a brief while Audrey had accepted Larry's hypothesis as preferable to the alternative that had occurred to her. But the more she thought, the less likely it appeared that Lord Hardcastle would ever part with such a valuable piece of jewelry. And certainly not anonymously. No, there was only one conclusion. "Will you tell Lord Elliott that I must see him at his earliest convenience?" she asked the maid who brought her breakfast chocolate.

She was dressed and had been pacing the room

for several minutes when a soft knock sounded. "Happy Christmas," Elliott said gravely after he had closed the door behind him. "You wished to see me?"

"Yes. I must return this." Audrey held up the jewel box.

"To me?" His feigned surprise lacked any conviction. "I really don't understand."

"Of course you do. And believe me when I say I am grateful. But I could never accept such a gift from you."

"You think *I* gave you the necklace? As much as I'd like to claim credit for such beneficence, the truth is—"

She placed her fingers on his lips. "The truth is, you are an abysmal liar."

"Oh, come now. You are letting your imagination run away with you, m'dear. Lawrence thinks Hardcastle sent it. He is most likely right."

"Stop it. We both know the truth. And while I think this is the kindest, most quixotic gesture imaginable . . ." She choked a bit. "I cannot permit it. Besides," she rallied, "it is no longer necessary." She thrust the necklace into his hands.

"Ah, yes, the pearls. They should more than pay your debt. Very well then." He shrugged and slipped the case inside his coat. "How did you know?" he asked her.

"I just did."

The memory of the moment beneath the mistletoe intruded in her thoughts. She tried to dismiss it. "The muff, of course, was a dead giveaway."

"I collect I did appear something of a skinflint."

"Well, now you can give the necklace to its rightful recipient."

"I can?" he answered dryly. "And just how do I explain myself?"

"You might say that the package got put with mine by mistake."

"I see. And that my hand just slipped when I wrote your name on the card in place of Regina's?"

"Oh."

" 'Oh' just about covers it."

"You will simply have to tell her the truth then. That you were trying to rescue me from ruin."

"And just what might she conclude from that?" he asked softly.

"That you have an excess of family feeling, perhaps, for your soon-to-be relations-in-law."

"Oh, I have an excess of feeling, all right." His voice was husky as he moved toward her. "But I do not think it is at all familial."

She wanted to put up a resistance when he took her in his arms. She found, however, to her deep chagrin, that she was incapable of such lofty character.

Chapter
Twenty-one

THE SLIDE WAS IN A DEEP GULLY THAT CUT THROUGH the park's woodlands where leftover stagnant water had frozen hard as iron. The servants had swept it clean of debris. There were signs of trampling where the young people of the Stonebridge staff had descended the steep incline and stamped their feet in the cold as they awaited their turns to slide.

"Oooh, famous!" Fitz crowed as he looked down at the long, smooth stretch of ice.

"It is that," Larry conceded. "Hey, wait a minute, let me hold the drum."

He was too late. Fitz had already started down the bank at a reckless speed that gathered more momentum as he went. The captain held his breath, but somehow boy and drum made it to the bottom without a calamity. It did occur to Larry as he scrambled down that he might have got a medal from the residents of the park had young Fitz indeed landed on his instrument and smashed it.

"Do you know how to do this?"

"Of course," Fitz replied haughtily. "Peter told me just how it is done." He shrugged out of the shoulder strap, cocked his elbows, took a running start, slid, wobbled, shrieked, and finished up the course scooting on his bottom.

"It ain't funny a bit," he said huffily when he regained his feet and saw his companion bent over with laughter.

"Sorry. But from here it is."

"Think you can do better?"

"Oh, lord, I hope so. Please observe. If I recall the technique, this figure is called 'knocking at the cobbler's door.'"

The captain took a running start, rather more cautiously than Fitz had done, then went gliding down the ice on one foot, occasionally giving a postman's knock with the other.

"Jiminy!" Fitz breathed in admiration.

"Ah, the old technique remains. Once mastered, not to be forgot. Now you try a slide. Only with both feet, please. One in front of the other works best."

This time Fitz remained upright for the entire course. And with a whoop he ran back beside the ice to try again. Soon they were taking turns, gliding like experts. The captain's slides were by far the more dramatic, due not so much to his one-foot technique but to the fact that Fitz accompanied him each time with deafening drumrolls.

At the end of one tricky maneuver, which involved a revolution midslide, Larry glanced up to see a rosy-cheeked, bright-eyed, hooded face gazing mockingly down at them from the bank. "Children must play, I see," Regina observed.

"Well, well, well. You found us."

"That was hardly difficult, was it? Between that deafening racket"—she nodded toward the drum—"and 'Over the Hills and Far Away' being bellowed out at the top of your lungs, I don't doubt they heard you in London."

"Well, someone has to have the Christmas spirit. Come join us if you dare."

"Of course I dare. There doesn't seem to be all that much to it." She scrambled down the bank, then, giving him a challenging look, took three quick, starting steps and began to slide in his direction.

Perhaps it was the sudden drum rumble that upset her equilibrium. Or perhaps it was the concern on the captain's face. But for whatever reason Miss Fielding's feet went out from underneath her and she finished the slide ignominiously prone.

Strong arms picked her up just as she was about to collide with a pair of Hessian boots. The arms clasped her to a caped greatcoat with rather more pressure and for a longer duration than seemed necessary. "Are you hurt?"

"No, except for the fact that you are squeezing the breath out of me."

"Oh, sorry." He held her at arm's length. "May I make a suggestion?"

"I am sure you will."

"If you were less attached to your Christmas present"—he was eyeing her muff critically—"you could use both hands for balance."

"Oh, but I'm not at all attached to my Christmas gift. In fact, I returned it to the Stonebridge library where it came from. A mistake, I now see. I might have attached it to my bottom as a precaution." She rubbed that part of her anatomy gingerly.

"Oh, yes. *Roderick Random*. I apologize for that.

It was a mean-spirited gesture made in a fit of the sulks because I could not hope to compete with diamonds and emeralds."

"Hey, move, would you!" Fitz yelled as he slid toward them. Larry obligingly lifted Regina to one side.

"It's your turn," the boy said when he'd halted.

"Never mind. Miss Fielding and I need to talk. You go ahead."

"Famous!" Fitz ran back to the starting place.

"We do not need to talk."

"Oh, yes, we do. For starters, tell me, how does it feel to discover suddenly that the man you don't love doesn't love you either?"

"There is nothing sudden about it. I have always known that Elliott doesn't love me."

"You have?" He gaped at her. "I'll not believe it."

"Well, you can believe it. He likes me very well. And is certain that I will make a most acceptable wife. But, no, he does not love me."

"Did he say as much?"

"Of course not. What kind of cad do you take him for?"

"Then what makes you think—"

"It is just something you know instinctively."

"I see." Larry looked at her thoughtfully. "By comparison, no doubt. Having been exposed to the real article, to wit, a man who does love you . . ."

Her already rosy cheeks colored a bit more. "Whee!" Fitz whooped as he went sailing past them, then hurried back again to the starting point.

"There was no comparison involved. Lord Elliott and I respect each other."

"Respect!" he scoffed.

"Yes, we do respect each other," she reaffirmed.

"And we should deal well together. Everyone says so. So when he proposed, naturally I accepted."

"Ah, yes. But that was before he fell in love with someone else."

She looked up at him steadily. "Are you really sure of what you are saying, or are you just trying to get back at me?"

"Oh, I am reasonably sure. As sure as one ever is about someone else's feelings. For I have learned that there's no absolute way to know what goes on in someone else's heart."

"Yes, I can see where you would have difficulty. It must be hard enough to deal with your own fickleness."

"Fickleness? Me? I was never fickle. And I was referring to *your* heart. That is, if you still have one. I had thought I knew it very well. But it seems I was wrong. So maybe I am also wrong about your fiancé and my stepmother. But, even so, as a detached impartial observer I would say they definitely love each other.

"Oops! Excuse me." He went to pick up Fitz, who had just gone sliding by on his stomach. "Now, then, where were we?" he asked after dusting off the lad and sending him on his way.

"You were saying you didn't really know whether Audrey and Elliott are in love."

"I was? Well, that's certainly a loose translation. But *you* tell *me*. You saw that kiss under the mistletoe. And at the time you looked as if you found it rather more than friendly."

"True. And there is the necklace. *My* necklace."

"Uh, well. As to the necklace . . ." The captain struggled with his conscience and then sighed. "As much as I hate saying it, there could be another explanation for that. I expect he felt the need to res-

169

cue her." He then went on to tell her the whole story.

Her eyes grew wide. "Aunt Audrey a gamester? I'll not believe it."

"Then don't," he snapped. "One stupid mistake does not a gamester make."

"It is in the blood though," she mused. "At least Mama was always pointing to her father as a horrible example."

"Sir Jervis is a horrible example, all right. But of gambling? Must not have been too addicted. He still has Stonebridge Park."

"Maybe it was a mere passing phase. All I know is that Mama says he and my grandmother used to have terrible rows about his gaming. They would not speak for days. And of course my uncle Chalgrove was notorious. But Audrey?"

"I hardly think Audrey is addicted. I know that she has been through hell over the episode, and I am not sure I shall ever forgive Danforth for allowing her to suffer. Like you, he has taken this 'Brougham curse' thing far too seriously."

Miss Fielding was deep in thought. "Still, as you say, this does rather put a different light on Elliott's gift."

"It does?" He looked uneasy.

"Oh, yes. There is no doubt that he would be concerned for her. They go back for years, you know. She was his sister's dearest friend. And Elliott is very chivalrous."

"I'm sure. Has a regular place at the Round Table, I wouldn't doubt."

"No need to—" Regina stopped abruptly to listen. "Oh, my goodness! Hear the church bells? I'd no idea it was so late."

"Do we have to go?" Fitz's face was long.

"Indeed we do," she replied firmly. "Our mutual

grandfather says it is most important that the Brougham pew be filled."

"Why?"

"Because he says so. Come on. We'd best hurry."

With the exception of Judith Fielding, who had insisted on the carriage being ordered out, the others had elected to walk to the church, situated a mile beyond the Stonebridge Park land. Regina, Larry, and Fitz hurried to catch up. Larry gave Regina a significant look when they first caught sight of their party.

Prayer book in hand, Anne Welbourne led the way, sandwiched between Danforth and Chalgrove. The latter was claiming her attention. He appeared to be talking with great animation while his lordship stared straight ahead.

But it was the laggards that Larry called attention to. Audrey and Elliott walked some distance behind the others. Their heads were close together in earnest conversation. Their hands were almost, but not quite, touching.

"Platonic, would you say?" The captain grinned.

"You have no call to enjoy this so much."

"Oh, have I not? Now you, too, can know what rejection's like."

"What are you two whispering about now?" Fitz demanded.

"Nothing to interest you, brat."

"Well, then, hurry up. I want to tell Papa about the slide." He beat a rousing tattoo on his drum that stopped the vanguard in its tracks. "Wait up, Papa," he whooped, and went racing toward them.

As they entered the grave-filled churchyard and walked up the path that led to the entrance of the ancient gray-stone, square-towered edifice, Chalgrove took charge of his offspring's drum. While they bobbed their heads respectfully, the villagers tried unsuccessfully to hide their smiles at the sight of the red instrument.

Somehow the family sorted itself out when they reached the enclosure that had been reserved for the Broughams since the fifteenth century. Judith Fielding was already ensconced there, a pious look firmly fixed on her face. Regina joined her, followed by Lord Elliott. Chalgrove ushered in Anne, leaving Lord Hunt to squire his stepmama.

Captain Hunt sighed as he found himself saddled with Master Brougham. His first task was to shush Fitz's "Jiminy!" when he spied an ancient tomb beside the altar with the effigy of a knight in armor prone upon it.

"Who's that?" the boy stage-whispered.

"One of your ancestors."

"Jiminy! Do you think it's Sir Gawain?"

"Probably."

"Jiminy! Why are his legs crossed?"

"Shows he was in the Crusades. Now be quiet."

The vicar had taken his place behind a pulpit piled so high with holly that little more of him could be seen than his grizzled wig and a pair of spectacles. He preached earnestly and at great length in defense of celebrating Christmas, supporting the correctness of his viewpoint with the opinions of various saints of the early church and demolishing the misguided piety of the Puritans, who had outlawed the observance two centuries before.

Perhaps because he was preaching to the converted, his rhetoric was wasted. At least no one seated in the Brougham pew had any desire to attack the holiday and were thus able to let their minds wander to more pressing problems. And so the sermon droned on, unheeded. Except for Captain Hunt, who was jerked back into the present, mid-homily. He was roused just in time to prevent Master Brougham from carving the remainder of his name in the bench between them. There was, alas, nothing he could do about the shaky, backward letter *F*.

Chapter
Twenty-two

S IR JERVIS HAD MADE IT CLEAR THAT CHRISTMAS DIN-
ner would be the climax of the Christmas visit.
He expected his nearest and dearest to leave the
park on the following day.

Dressed with unusual care, he honored the occasion by taking his place at the head of the festive
board. His evening clothes were not of the latest
crack and had taken on the patina of age, but he
still managed to cut a dashing figure.

His elder daughter said as much. "You are looking very handsome, Father."

"Thank you." The voice sounded half pleased,
half sardonic. "You are quite grand yourself, Judith. I see you are wearing the famous necklace."

Mrs. Fielding's hand flew to her throat, perhaps
for reassurance. "I have scarcely had it off since its
mysterious return. I shall probably sleep in it tonight in case our prankster decides to repeat his

little joke." While she spoke she looked pointedly at Fitz.

"And you, Audrey," Sir Jervis continued, "are also adorned, I see." She was wearing her new pearl necklace over a low-cut lilac gown. "Very lovely. But how did you make a choice between your Christmas jewels?"

Without waiting for a reply, he stared his granddaughter's way. "Perhaps you should have lent Regina your diamonds. Her throat seems a bit too bare." His wicked chuckle earned him some uneasy and resentful glances. It seemed that Sir Jervis missed very little.

There was scant conversation during the meal. The host turned his full attention to the soup, fish, turkey, goose, sweetbreads, chicken, beef collops, lamb, neat's tongue, rabbits, and mutton and the various vegetables and desserts that made up the feast. And except for a few remarks made in appreciation of certain succulent dishes, the others followed his example. It was only after they were completely sated with plum pudding and/or minced pie that Sir Jervis picked up his heavy silver knife and tapped it against a crystal goblet for their attention.

"Have a few remarks to make," he bellowed down the table. "Won't stand up to make 'em. Legs not what they used to be. Think you all can hear me."

"They can hear you in China, Papa," Chalgrove said cheerfully over his wineglass.

"Humph! Want to thank you all for humoring me by coming. We ain't lively here like in the metropolis—though we did have our moments, I collect." He chuckled as he looked at first one and then another of his guests, all of whom appeared to be made uncomfortable by his scrutiny. "This is my last Christmas, I expect." He waved away the demurring murmurs. "I wanted it to be one you'd not forget. And I daresay you won't." Again he chuckled. "Also I wished to put me house in order before I shuffle off this mortal coil—that's Shakespeare, lad!" he shouted down the table to Fitz, who looked back blankly, unimpressed.

"First of all, I want to make it clear that I am leaving everything I have to me only son." His gimlet eyes fastened on Chalgrove, who took a deep and noisy gulp of port. There was a dramatic pause. "On one condition." No one seemed to breathe. "On one condition," Sir Jervis repeated. "That he marry Anne here. As soon as possible."

Chalgrove choked. Anne looked aghast. Danforth leaped to his feet. "Now see here. This is not the Middle Ages. You can't barter Miss Welbourne off like chattel!"

"Audrey, tell that young whelp to stay out of what don't concern him," Sir Jervis barked. "Now then, Chalgrove," he continued as Audrey tugged at Danforth's sleeve until he resumed his seat, "what do you have to say for yourself? I'm ready to forgive and forget on that one condition. I can't say fairer. Anne is a pearl above price and will be a tip-top mother to the lad there."

Fitz's eyes were saucer-wide. "Does he really want you to marry Miss Welbourne, Papa? Mama won't like that one little bit."

"He's right, you know." Chalgrove was wiping the wine from his lapels, where he'd sprayed it. "Nothing against Anne here. She is all you say, and more." The look he gave Anne was a bit regretful and slightly lecherous. "But the fact is, it won't do. There's the matter of bigamy, you see. Fact is, I'm already married."

"To Mama," Fitz chimed in.

It was Sir Jervis's turn to sputter. "But you told me you were not married."

"Oh, no, sir. Beg pardon. Couldn't have done. Oh!" Chalgrove snapped his fingers as the light dawned. "Believe I did say I did not marry the opera dancer. Wouldn't've dreamed of doing such a thing."

"Then who?" his father thundered.

"Lady Maureen Fitzpatrick. Fine woman. Top of the trees. You'd all like her." He beamed around the table. "Her father's Lord Fitzpatrick of County Cork."

"Not the horse Fitzpatrick!" Larry blurted out.

"The very one. Biggest breeder in Ireland."

"And the richest."

"Oh, yes. Regular nabob, in fact. Maureen's his only child. Horse-mad herself. That's why she didn't come with me. Her favorite mare's about to foal."

"You mean to tell me that you have married a fortune?" Sir Jervis's eyes were bugging.

"Well, I dislike being so crass, but yes."

"My God!"

"Then it scarcely seems necessary to leave him everything, does it?" Mrs. Fielding observed.

"Oh, I'd be quite happy to inherit. Give me a bit of a boost in his horsy lordship's eyes. He wasn't best pleased when Maureen took me with nothing beyond me smallclothes. Of course, he couldn't kick up too much of a dust." He winked at the company. "She was *enceinte*, you see."

"What's that?" Fitz inquired.

"Never you mind."

"So Fitz is named for his Irish grandfather," Audrey said hastily. "Under the circumstances, that was tactful of you."

"No he ain't. His full name is Jervis Chalgrove

Kelly Brougham. We just called him Fits because he throws so many. Maureen's the only one who can handle him. A most determined female. It's the same with the horses."

"Well, I'm damned," Sir Jervis breathed. "You named the brat for me."

"There goes the inheritance, Mama." Regina giggled.

"Seems to me you should leave some jewelry to Audrey, though," Chalgrove said magnanimously. "Only fair. Judith's necklace must be worth a fortune."

"Think so, do you?" The old man snorted. "Shows how little you know. Any of you, for that matter. Though I must say it's an excellent copy. Top of the trees, in fact."

There was a thunderous silence. Mrs. Fielding's hands flew to her neck as though to shield her jewels from this terrible accusation.

"Are you saying that Mama's necklace is a fake, that you had the real one copied?"

Regina asked the question her mother could not utter.

"*I* didn't have it copied. Your grandmother did. It was the last piece of the family jewels. The others had been turned into paste one by one to pay her gambling debts. She'd given her solemn oath not to touch this one. It was the prize of the collection. But she could no more stay away from the faro table than you can keep a rooster out of the henhouse. I wondered why she was so anxious on her deathbed to give the necklace away. That's why I borrowed the thing to have it appraised. Hoped to be proved wrong, but I wasn't."

"Are you saying Mama gambled?" Audrey stared in disbelief.

Her father nodded. "Regular addict, in fact."

"But I . . . we . . . thought—"

"That it was me? I know. High time the record was set straight. Lucy's father had the same weakness. I believed I was marrying a fortune, but as it worked out—well, never mind. Always worried, though, that one of you would inherit the curse. But I trust," he said dryly, "that whatever lapses any of you may have had were only temporary aberrations.

"But enough of this. Except for that weakness, your mother was a fine, upstanding woman. But now you know, Audrey, why I could not give you any of the Brougham jewelry. The collection was wiped out years ago. You can restore the copies if you wish, Chalgrove. I never bothered."

"Hmmm. We'll see. Actually, Maureen has all the baubles she can manage. Still, for the family name . . ."

He lapsed into silence, apparently thinking the matter over.

Regina cleared her throat. "Since this seems to be the occasion for dropping bombshells, I have an announcement to make. Lord Elliott and I are calling off our engagement."

There was a crash. Elliott, having no bomb at hand, had dropped his water goblet.

"Regina!" Mrs. Fielding's voice was terrible. "Your jest is in the poorest possible taste."

"I'm not funning, Mama. Elliott and I have decided that we would not suit." She gave her erstwhile fiancé a shaky smile as he gaped at her. "It is nothing personal. We remain the best of friends, do we not, Elliott?"

Too dumbfounded to speak, he managed a nod. Captain Hunt, on the other hand, had broken into a delighted grin. He raised his wineglass. "To friendship," he murmured, and then drained it.

Mrs. Fielding appeared close to apoplexy. "You cannot be throwing away a superb catch like Lord Elliott for that ... that ..."—she glared the captain's way—"here-and-thereian."

"Captain Hunt has nothing to say in the matter. This is purely between Lord Elliott and myself."

"Then why is he the last to know it?" Sir Jervis chuckled.

"I expect she's in a pucker over the necklace," Master Jervis Chalgrove Kelly Brougham explained to the group at large. "Lord Elliott brought it for *her*"—he pointed to Regina—"then gave it to *her*." The index finger singled out the Dowager Lady Hunt.

Her sister gave a pathetic moan and fainted.

Chapter
Twenty-three

"GO AWAY!"

Regina had opened her door in response to a brisk knock. Now she tried to slam it shut. But Captain Hunt's evening slipper got in the way.

"Ouch! Dammit, don't be so rough. You could cripple a fellow." He pushed his way in, closed the door behind him, and came directly to the point. "Miss Fielding, will you do me the honor of becoming my bride? Oops, I forgot the drill." He dropped to one knee, grinned up at her, and repeated the question.

"You don't seem to grasp the situation." She stared down at him stonily. "I don't wish to talk to you, let alone marry you. I have just had a scene with my mother that has left me with a severe megrim."

"Oh, you poor, poor thing." He clucked soothingly as he rose and took her tenderly in his arms. "You have to understand her point of view. Losing

Elliott—and to Audrey, of all people—is a severe blow. But she'll get over it. And I'm not all that bad a catch. I'm only a second son by fifteen minutes. And I'm to have the estate in Hampshire. That will keep us comfortable even without your considerable fortune, though I would much prefer to be more than comfortable with it."

"I repeat," she said coldly, "I have no intention of accepting your offer."

"Oh, yes, you have." He nibbled tenderly at her ear.

"Well, certainly not for a long, long time," she gasped as his lips moved down her neck. "If you want me, you'll have to, by George, woo me."

"And just what the devil do you think I'm doing?" He paused in his pursuit to ask.

"I mean for *ages*. Flowers, bonbons, with lots and lots of groveling thrown in."

"Sorry, I can't comply. Oh, not that I wouldn't enjoy the process," he hastened to say as she tried to wriggle out of his grasp, "but we haven't that much time."

"We have all the time in the world," she countered.

"Well, *we* might have. But Audrey and Elliott, at their advanced ages, haven't. We will have to marry first, of course. It would never do for it to look as though Elliott had thrown you over."

"Is that what people will think?" She was horrified.

"Actually, no, for Audrey will refuse to marry until you are wed. Think about it. You do see her position, don't you? Not to mention your mother's. You'll simply have to make the sacrifice of a hurry-up ceremony to save face all around."

He clasped her tighter. His lips resumed their roving. The strength of his arguments prevailed.

182

Miss Fielding's attitude underwent a sea change. She grew quite cooperative, in fact. At least up to the point where he began to fumble with the fasteners of her gown. "Stop it!" she hissed, and gave him a shove. "Control yourself. You've made your point. We'll have an early wedding."

"We could leave for Gretna Green tonight," he suggested hopefully.

"Don't be daft. Mama would never speak to us again."

The captain's eyes lit for a moment as he allowed himself to dwell on such a prospect. His prudent nature prevailed, however. "We'll wait, then." He sighed. "But, mind you, not for long. Forget all those other reasons that I mentioned. The fact is, I am simply not able to."

He enfolded her in his arms once more.

When Anne Welbourne entered Sir Jervis's bedchamber early the following morning, she found the baronet standing by the window staring down at the circular driveway.

"I came to see if you needed me for anything," she said when she had joined him. He was watching Lady Hunt being helped into her carriage by her soldier stepson, who then climbed in beside her. Young Fitz, drum-adorned, stood watching.

"Well, there they go." The baronet chuckled. "Fancy Audrey, at her age, being able to snatch Elliott right out from under me hoity-toity daughter's nose."

"Don't you mean your granddaughter's nose, sir?"

"No. I meant what I just said. It was Judith who was dead set on the match. The breakup prostrated her, didn't it? But there was no need for her to scream at Audrey like a fishwife. That wedding never would have taken place. Knew that the minute Lawrence Hunt came limping in here wearing that eye patch. He was determined to have Regina. And he'd have got her even without Audrey's help or I'm a Dutchman."

"But as it was, things did work out well, did they not, sir? Lord Elliott and Audrey are obviously very much in love. Did you know he'd had a *tendre* for her ever since she was in boarding school?"

"I know that all young men are fools. The only good thing about old age is that you get beyond that kind of nonsense."

From below them came the roll of a drum. Lady Hunt's coachman sprang the horses and the carriage swept around the drive accompanied by Fitz's cadence and his shouts of farewell.

"Regular little limb of Satan, ain't he?" his grandfather remarked admiringly.

"Oh, he's a grandson to be proud of. I'll wager you never expected that kind of bonus when you arranged the reconciliation with Chalgrove."

He turned to glare down at her. "I arranged nothing. Chalgrove just decided it was time to mend his fences, that's all."

"Fustian. He got a Christmas invitation just like the others. And one that *I* never wrote. You'll not convince me that getting him here was not the object of this exercise."

"If you must know, missy, finding you a husband was the object of this exercise. And, by gad"—he chuckled—"looks like I fixed that, too. Not in the way I'd hoped, mind you, but I must admit that Hunt's a far better catch than Chalgrove. A dull dog. But you'll probably like that."

"Lord Hunt is certainly not dull," she retorted. "But you take far too much for granted if you think him likely to offer for me."

"Demmed if I do. Why else would he ask to stay

on a few days in this mausoleum? Not for the pleasure of my company, that's certain. For I told him plain out that he could stay as long as I didn't have to see him."

"How hospitable," she murmured.

"Well, it was, in fact, considering I'm ready to see the backsides of everybody." He turned from the window and limped goutily toward his bed. "All this playing Cupid takes it out of a cove. Let's see now. . . . We've made a match with Audrey and Elliott, Regina and Lawrence, you and Hunt. What's more, me scapegrace son has found himself an Irish heiress and produced an offspring who'll be my vengeance for every gray hair he ever cost me.

"Yes, it's been as good as a play to watch the business unfold. Who knows," he said as he climbed unaided onto the high four-poster and sank back against the pillows with a sigh, "I may decide to take to me deathbed again next Christmas to see how it all turns out."